COUNT DOWN

JANUARY

by
Daniel Parker

Simon & Schuster
www.SimonSays.com/countdown/

To Jessica

First Aladdin Paperbacks edition December 1998

Produced by 17th Street Productions,
a division of Daniel Weiss Associates, Inc.

Aladdin Paperbacks
An imprint of Simon & Schuster
Children's Publishing Division
1230 Avenue of the Americas
New York, NY 10020

Library of Congress Cataloging-in-Publication Data
Parker, Daniel, 1970–
January / Daniel Parker. — 1st Aladdin Paperbacks ed.
p. cm. — (Countdown ; 1)
Summary: New Year's Day 1999 brings a strange solar flare, widescale
power outages, and the death of everyone on Earth over twenty years old,
leaving desperate teenagers to face the awkward demon called Lilith.
ISBN 0-689-81819-X (pbk.)
[1. Supernatural—Fiction.] I. Title.
II. Series: Parker, Daniel, 1970– Countdown ; 1.
PZ7.P2243Jan   1998
[Fic]—dc21   98-7692
CIP   AC

"YOU MUST FIND THE SCROLL . . ."

"The scroll," the old man croaked. There was a gurgling noise in his throat, as if he were drowning. "The code is hidden in the scroll. Use the code." He shot her a crazed look. His face was soaking wet.

"*Find* it!" he hissed.

"Elijah, just take it easy," she soothed—as much for herself as for her granduncle. "We'll get the driver to pull over." She reached out to touch her uncle's shoulder, to reassure him.

His jacket felt strangely warm.

She pushed the material harder. His clothing seemed to give a little, as if the flesh underneath the fabric wasn't solid. She stopped breathing. Something was pulsating unevenly under there . . . it didn't feel right. Her hand involuntarily flinched away from him.

"Unc-Uncle Elijah?" she stammered, unable to keep the fear out of her voice.

He didn't answer.

Sarah clamped her hands over her mouth. Her eyes widened. Elijah wasn't merely sick; he was *diseased*. His skin was splotchy. Horrid black blisters welled up on his cheeks. He scratched at his face, tearing the flesh. It came off in bloody chunks on his fingertips.

"*Stop the bus!*" Sarah screamed, leaping out of her seat. "*Stop it!*"

But nobody was behind the wheel.

About the Author

Daniel Parker is the author of over twenty books for children and young adults. He lives in New York City with his wife, a dog, and a psychotic cat named Bootsie. He is a Leo. When he isn't writing, he is tirelessly traveling the world on a doomed mission to acheive rock-and-roll stardom. As of this date, his musical credits include the composition of bluegrass soundtrack numbers for the film *The Grave* (starring a bloated Anthony Michael Hall) and a brief stint performing live rap music to baffled Filipino audiences in Hong Kong. Mr. Parker once worked in a cheese shop. He was fired.

PROLOGUE

10:55 a.m., January 1, 1999 (8:55 a.m. Greenwich Mean Time)
Secret Russian Military Installation at Poulostrov Kanin,
North of Arctic Circle

Colonel Yuri Petrovich stood on the tiny wooden platform of the lookout tower, staring once again across the shadowy, frozen wasteland that stretched before him.

There was nothing to see, of course. Even in the summer months, when the sun managed to skirt above the horizon, there was nothing to see. In the five years that he'd been here, the view had remained perfectly stagnant—like a bad photograph.

The door behind him opened and slammed. Yuri groaned quietly. He wasn't in the mood to chat.

"Good morning, Colonel," said a cheery young voice in the darkness.

Yuri didn't bother to reply. He absently fingered the launch keys on the chain around his neck. *Good morning?* he asked himself with a scowl. What was good about it? What was *good* about being stuck a few hundred kilometers from the North Pole in the dead of winter? What was so damn good about guarding a pile of rusted metal—

"And happy New Year," the voice added.

Yuri sighed. His breath formed an icy cloud

1

against the starless sky. New Year's Day always put him in a foul mood. Particularly in this dismal place. He turned and glanced at the scrawny soldier, bundled in combat boots and a thick white snowsuit, a machine gun slung over his shoulder.

Foolish boy, Yuri couldn't help but think. It was Nikolai Militov: a new arrival, barely twenty years old. Yuri knew that Nikolai was thrilled to be stationed here—where the temperature never rose above freezing, where the sun set for the last time in November and didn't rise again until February. After all, it was an honor to serve at Poulostrov Kanin. The high command in Moscow wouldn't even tell them what they were guarding. The weapons here were *that* secret. Not even Yuri knew. Ah, no . . . but Yuri knew one thing. He knew that Nikolai was in for a big surprise. The thrill of the top secret assignment would wear off soon enough. Frostbite, boredom, and depression would take its place.

Nikolai cleared his throat. "Private Pushkin and I wanted to know if you wanted to join us for a drink in the launch center, sir," he stated.

Yuri regarded him for a moment. In the buzzing fluorescent light Nikolai's pockmarked skin looked deathly pale—except for his nose, which had already turned red. The boy looked terrible. Then again, Yuri supposed that he himself didn't look much better. At least Nikolai was young. Yuri, on the other hand . . .

Nikolai flashed a nervous, yellow grin. "A toast to celebrate the New Year—"

"You want me to *abandon* my *post?*" Yuri interrupted.

2

Nikolai's grin vanished. "N-no, sir," he stammered. "I just . . ."

No sense of humor, Yuri thought grimly. *He doesn't get it.* Did Nikolai truly believe that they *needed* to protect this forgotten dump? From whom? Russia no longer had enemies. Russia wasn't important enough to have enemies.

"I'm teasing," Yuri murmured, forcing a tired smile. "You'll have to forgive my strange sense of humor. Yes, I could use a drink right now. Thank you."

Nikolai nodded, then breathed a quick sigh of relief. He opened the door. Yuri hurried into the worn spiral stairwell, overcome with the sudden loneliness he always felt when he'd been misunderstood. The older he got, the less people seemed to understand him. Yes, he *did* need a drink right now. Badly.

"You know, it's nearly eleven in the morning," Yuri commented, pausing at the steel door at the bottom of the steps. "Aren't we supposed to raise our glasses at the stroke of midnight?"

"It's midnight somewhere, sir," Nikolai replied.

Yuri chuckled. So the boy *did* have a sense of humor after all. "Spoken like a true Russian alcoholic," he muttered. He punched the fifteen-digit security code into a grid of numbers next to the door, then stood back as the door hissed open and locked in place. He didn't bother closing it. Why should he? It was too much of a hassle. Besides, he was here to get drunk, not worry about meaningless security procedures.

"Comrade Colonel!" Private Sasha Pushkin

bellowed drunkenly from inside the launch center. "Happy New Year!"

Yuri smirked. The young man was sprawled across the drab concrete floor, half out of his snow-suit, his head propped against a bank of outdated computers. His black eyes were glazed. A grubby, half-finished bottle of generic vodka stood at his side.

"Looks like somebody began the party without us," Yuri remarked dryly. He glanced back at Nikolai. Nikolai shrugged.

"Sorry, Comrade Colonel," Sasha mumbled.

Yuri took a step forward and snatched the bottle off the floor. "Why do you insist on calling me 'comrade' anyway, Private Pushkin?" he asked. His tone was playful. "I haven't been called comrade in over eight years."

Sasha belched, then hiccuped. "Respect, sir," he slurred.

"Respect?" Yuri snickered, raising his bushy eyebrows. "For what?"

"For the cold war!" Sasha proclaimed. "For communism! For the days of the Soviet Union, when the whole world trembled at our feet!"

Yuri's smile dissolved. He raised the bottle to his lips. Ah, yes . . . how bright the future had seemed in the heady days of the cold war! He took a long slug of vodka, wincing as the bitter liquid plunged into his empty stomach—*bam!* . . . then relaxing as ripples of warmth spread through his body. His eyes grew misty. All that remained of the Soviet Union were crumbling and obsolete bases like this one: pitiful monuments to the glorious

4

days of the past. Did anyone even *remember* what kind of secret weapons sat idling here?

"Happy New Year, Comrade Colonel," Sasha said dully.

Yuri took another gulp. "Happy New Year," he echoed. "May we all—" He broke off in midsentence.

The lights had gone out. Just like that.

So much for getting drunk, Yuri thought. One moment he was in the midst of a toast; the next he was standing in pitch-blackness like an idiot. He couldn't see a damn thing. It was as if somebody had draped an inky velvet hood over his head. "Perfect," he groaned. "Another power failure."

Sasha giggled in the dark.

"What should we do, sir?" Nikolai asked anxiously.

"Don't be so nervous, Nik," Sasha chided. "We lose power all the time. The lines freeze and collapse. You'll get used to it."

Yuri shifted the vodka bottle to his left hand and groped for the walkie-talkie on his belt. "The best thing to do is to stay right here," he said. "I'll contact the patrol and instruct them to locate the problem." After a few seconds of fumbling, his gloved fingers wrapped around the familiar plastic shape. He lifted the walkie-talkie to his lips and flicked the switch.

"Unit one, do you read?" he asked.

There was no response. Not even the crackle of static.

"Unit one?" he repeated, frowning.

Silence.

Yuri's eyes narrowed. The walkie-talkie wasn't working. He flicked the switch again, but the speaker emitted no sound. There *should* have been static. . . .

"Can't raise them, sir?" Sasha asked.

"No, no—it's not that," Yuri murmured distractedly. "I think the walkie-talkie is dead."

There was a pause.

"Dead?" Sasha asked. The word was clipped. He no longer sounded drunk. "Is it the battery, Colonel?"

Yuri tried the switch one last time. He licked his dry lips. He suddenly felt light-headed. It couldn't be the battery. He'd changed the battery yesterday.

"Is it the battery, sir?" Nikolai demanded.

"No."

For a moment the black room was perfectly silent. Yuri's pulse quickened. Sasha and Nikolai must have been thinking the same thing: Only one phenomenon could kill the power in the launch center *and* in the walkie-talkie. Only one. A powerful electromagnetic pulse. The kind caused by an explosion of some sort—

"That sound!" Nikolai whispered.

Yuri held his breath.

What the . . .

Nikolai was right; there *was* a sound. Something that drifted in and out of the wind. It sounded sweet and high-pitched, like . . . like . . .

"Singing," Sasha croaked. "A choir—"

"Sssh!" Nikolai hissed tremulously.

The sound faded. Yuri's mind began to race. It *was* singing. So that was a good sign. One of the patrolmen must have been listening to music. In that case the power outage *couldn't* have been

6

caused by an electromagnetic pulse. Maybe the walkie-talkie just happened to break at the exact same moment the power had failed. It was a coincidence, a fluke. The walkie-talkie was just another piece of poorly manufactured crap like everything else in this place. Besides, the chances were one in a billion that anyone would attack, right?

Yuri held his breath again.

Right?

As if the question demanded an answer, there was a faint *rat-tat-tat* of machine-gun fire.

The vodka bottle slipped from Yuri's fingers. It shattered on the floor.

"This can't be happening," Nikolai murmured in a ghastly voice. "It's—"

"Shut up!" Sasha barked.

Yuri whirled and stumbled past Nikolai. *A billion to one,* he thought desperately. He hurtled up the stairwell, then burst through the door onto the lookout platform. Freezing wind whipped at his face. The sky hung over him like an indigo blanket. He crouched by the guardrail and withdrew his revolver—but he felt oddly detached from the situation, as if he were dreaming. Then he peered over the side.

My God.

Dozens of shadows were moving swiftly and silently toward the entrance below. Of course: When the power had failed, the electric fence had failed, too. The base was wide open. Another burst of machine-gun fire tore through the dim half-light, followed by screams, then by a final shot—so close that it seemed to come from the bottom of the steps. Yuri's stomach squeezed. He couldn't focus. The situation was unraveling much too fast.

They've already penetrated, he realized. Blood drained from his face. *They've already reached the launch center. . . .*

He pivoted to face the door.

A silhouette was standing there.

I'm dead.

For the first time in his life Yuri was too frightened to react. He'd been in combat before, but this was different. He couldn't move. He couldn't breathe. His entire being—his senses, his thoughts, *everything*—had been reduced to a single conclusion: His life was over.

The silhouette drifted toward him. Amazingly enough, even in his petrified state Yuri was still able to admire how this *person,* this *attacker,* moved with such grace, like a ballet dancer. And the uniform . . . It was unlike any he'd ever seen—a loose, hooded black robe, not at all military. It seemed almost . . . *religious.*

"Who are you?" Yuri breathed. "What do you want?"

There was no response.

He had to move. His trembling fingers struggled to cock the pistol. To raise it toward the attacker's shrouded face—

His jaw dropped.

This isn't happening.

He was certain of that now. None of this was real.

It *couldn't* be real because the face didn't belong to a soldier. It belonged to a beautiful teenage girl . . . with slender cheekbones, full lips, smooth skin, and shiny dark eyes. She kicked the pistol from Yuri's loose grasp and in one deft maneuver swiped the launch keys from around his neck.

"Impossible," he murmured.

And then she was gone, back down the stairs to the launch center.

Yuri collapsed back against the guardrail. The wind burned his nose; his knuckles stung where he'd been kicked—but he knew that he was simply trapped in the throes of some vivid nightmare. Yes, he was even beginning to feel a peculiar sort of relief. In a moment he would wake up.

The sound of that sweet, hypnotic singing began to drift up through the stairwell. Yuri gaped blankly at the open door. What language was that? It sounded like gibberish. He listened carefully, but after a few seconds the song was drowned out by a deep, low rumble. The rumble grew until it filled Yuri's ears. The platform vibrated in sympathy. Yes—yes, of course: The weapons—*whatever* they might be—were being detonated. But how could they be detonated when the base had no power? *Ach* . . . it didn't matter. Yuri was no longer afraid. In fact, he almost smiled.

All a dream, he said to himself. *An absurd dream.*

He knew the absurd dream must have been responsible for the sudden prickling sensation creeping up his spine. It was responsible for the strange heat on the back of his neck, for the loss of moisture in his mouth, for the beads of sweat on his forehead.

He *was* hot, wasn't he?

All a dream.

No, he was more than hot. He was on fire. His breath came in quick, short gasps. Searing pain shot through his arms and legs. It spread to the very tips of his fingers and toes.

All a dream, he repeated to himself.

The words became a private mantra, a silent chant, repeated over and over again.

Panting, he peeled off his snowsuit jacket, his shirts, his thermal underwear—until nothing stood between his naked torso and the subzero Arctic air. Still he burned.

All a dream.

He stared down at his belly. The pudgy flesh there was puckering into thick black welts. It started falling off his body. Never before had he experienced such pain—never in his waking life. Blood bubbled forth, revealing hissing organs, blackened bones, charred arteries.

He was melting. From the inside out.

All a dream. All a—

PART I:

January 1, 1999
8:55 a.m. to 9:18 a.m. Greenwich Mean Time

CHAPTER
ONE

"This is where it gets *really* crazy. . . ."

Ariel Collins picked at the label of her empty beer bottle. She'd never been so bored. She was so bored, she thought she was going to *die* or something.

I can't believe Jez hasn't shut up yet.

No, actually she *could* believe it. Jezebel Howe hardly ever shut up. Ariel just couldn't believe she was wasting New Year's Eve, 1998—the biggest New Year's Eve of her entire seventeen-year-old life—listening to this garbage. Why couldn't she be somewhere else? Babylon was the worst. It wasn't even a real town. It was a *suburb*—a suburb of Seattle, no less. And as far as cities went, Seattle was pretty lame, too.

". . . so this guy guns the car up to like eighty-five, right?" Jezebel was saying. Her porcelain face glowed blue in the flickering light of the muted TV. "Meanwhile Brian is totally freaking out. He's all like, 'Slow down, man! We're gonna get killed. Or worse! We're gonna get arrested!'"

Jack laughed. *Again.* It didn't matter that he had heard the same dumb story at least a billion times already. It didn't matter that Jezebel was only telling the story to rag on Ariel's boyfriend, who happened to be passed out on the floor. Of course not. Jezebel was saying something that *she* thought was funny. *Somebody* in this living room had to provide the laugh track. And who better than her cheesy, twenty-year-old meathead boyfriend, Jack Grant?

"Anyway, I'm chilling in the backseat," Jezebel went on. She brushed her dyed black hair behind her ears, then dramatically eased back into the sofa—as if an actual demonstration of "chilling" were crucial to everyone's understanding of what happened. "But I'm starting to get nervous. You know that way Brian has of making people nervous—"

"Does anybody want more beer?" Ariel interrupted.

For an instant Jezebel's expression soured. Then she smiled again. "Can't you wait, like, ten seconds?"

"I'm thirsty," Ariel said. She pushed herself off the worn carpet and glanced at Brian, sprawled in a heap beside the beer-splattered coffee table. At least she had *him*. Even when Brian Landau was wasted, he was still hot. Of course, he didn't get wasted that often. So it was all the more cute when he did. That tousled blond hair, that ratty flannel shirt, those gorgeous blue eyes—closed now, obviously, due to massive amounts of alcohol and boredom . . . Ariel couldn't help but smile. She gently kicked the bottom of one of his Timberland boots.

"Psst, Bri," she whispered. "Wake up, sweetie. It's almost midnight."

Brian groaned. He sounded vaguely ill.

"So can I finish?" Jezebel grumbled.

Ariel rolled her eyes. "Oh, please do," she begged sarcastically. She stepped over Brian and headed for the kitchen. "I can't *wait* to hear what happens next. Did you all die?"

Jack snickered from the couch. "You're just embarrassed because *your* wuss boyfriend was the one who freaked out."

Ariel paused. She stared at him blankly. One word always leaped to mind when it came to Jack. *Thick.* That pretty much captured everything about him: his skull, obviously—but also the way he talked, his chest, his neck . . . even his hair. He looked as if he had brown steel wool glued to the top of his head.

"Jack, it's amazing," she said. "Those workouts are doing a lot more than making your muscles freakishly big. They're also reducing the size of your brain." With that she pushed through the swinging kitchen door—and nearly slammed into her brother, Trevor.

"Jesus!" she hissed angrily. "What are *you* doing here?"

Trevor didn't say anything. He just stared at her.

Ariel shuddered, then sidestepped him and opened the refrigerator. *Eww,* she thought. Her own brother gave her the willies. Her own brother! Did anybody else have that kind of problem? The scary thing was that she and Trevor *looked* so much alike, too. It was undeniable. He was two years older, but they could have been twins. They both had the same hazel eyes, the same straight brownish blond hair, the same slender frames . . . *yuck.* She couldn't think about it anymore. It was too depressing.

"I think Brian's had too much to drink," Trevor remarked.

"How would *you* know?" Ariel muttered. She grabbed a beer (her fifth? her sixth? She lost track after Brian suggested they both slow down)—then slammed the refrigerator door. "And why would you even care?" she asked. "You hate his guts, remember?"

"He's passed out on the rug," Trevor said simply. "I don't want him to puke on it."

Ariel turned and glared at him. Trevor always spoke in the same creepy, dull monotone. He sounded more like a machine than a person. But that would make sense. He spent his entire life staring at a computer screen. Oh, well. She twisted the cap off the bottle. It opened with a satisfying *thock*.

Here's to the year 1999, she silently toasted. The cap clattered to the floor. *May Whoever's-up-there grant me everything I want.*

She started guzzling.

Trevor sneered. "Dad's gonna kill you when he comes home."

"Look, why don't just go hang out with your geeky engineering-school friends or something?" Ariel suggested, pausing in midgulp. A few drops of beer spilled on her chin. She wiped them away with the sleeve of her gray wool sweater. "It's gotta beat hiding out in here and spying on us."

Trevor's jaw tightened. "I'm not spying. I came home to make sure you guys didn't trash the house—"

The door burst open.

Jezebel strode into the kitchen, looking annoyed.

15

She went straight for the refrigerator. She didn't even acknowledge Trevor's presence. Trevor, as usual, just stared at her. He might as well have been drooling.

"I think I *will* have a beer," Jezebel mumbled to nobody in particular.

"Tired of telling the same old story, Jez?" Ariel teased. She raised the bottle to her lips again.

"Nobody was listening," Jezebel stated glumly. Her long black dress swished as she moved. Jezebel owned at least a dozen black dresses, and they were all exactly the same. It was par for the course, though. The girl had discovered silver jewelry, the color black, and Marilyn Manson a few years before—and it had been all downhill from there.

"Maybe that's because Jack's heard the story before," Ariel muttered. "And Brian is totally out of it."

Jezebel laughed shortly. She snatched a beer off the shelf. "He looks happy, though, doesn't he?"

Ariel shrugged. "I'd be happy, too, if I'd had eighty beers."

Jezebel cast her a glance before closing the refrigerator door. "Looks like you're on your way. Is that your seventy-ninth?"

Trevor chuckled. Ariel pretended to ignore him. This conversation was none of his business anyway.

"Jezebel, please," she said dryly. She took another sip. "You sound like Brian did before he passed out."

"And that's bad?" Jezebel asked with an innocent smile. She opened her own bottle.

Ariel raised her eyebrows. "What's that supposed to mean?"

"You tell me," she replied in an easygoing tone, meeting Ariel's gaze. "I've never been able to figure you two out anyway. He's so nice and sweet and responsible—well, except for tonight—and you're so . . ." She swallowed some beer. "Besides, there must be a reason you're in here avoiding your boyfriend and getting sloshed with *him*." She jerked a thumb at Trevor.

Ariel laughed again, as casually as ever. If Jezebel actually thought she could provoke some kind of reaction with a cheap little jab like that . . . well, she was very, very wrong. "Funny," Ariel said. "I was just thinking the same thing about you and Jack. I've never been able to figure out why a hip goth-rocker like you would fall for such a jackass. Is it because he laughs at anything you say?"

Jezebel's smile didn't budge a millimeter. She didn't even blink.

"You know what, Ariel?" she asked sweetly. "I'm glad we're finally having this conversation. One of my New Year's resolutions is to be more open and honest with my best friend."

"Hey, Jezebel," Ariel whispered, leaning close. "We're not best friends. We're just two chicks who look good together in a crowd, remember?"

Jezebel glowered at her. Ariel suppressed a giggle. *Now* they were having some fun. Moments like these were what made hanging out with Jezebel so worthwhile: the crazy, tense times when neither of them knew who was bluffing—the times when both of them pushed and pushed. . . .

"You're drunk," Jezebel mumbled, turning away.

17

Ariel laughed delightedly. "Of course I am. It's New Year's Eve, babe!" She started singing in a loud, out-of-tune voice. *"And tonight I'm gonna party like it's nineteen ninety—"*

"You guys!" Jack called from the living room. "Get in here! The countdown is starting!"

"Whoopee," Jezebel muttered. She trudged back through the door. Trevor followed.

Ariel allowed herself another little laugh. Jezebel was all flustered and out of sorts. Well, she should have known better than to play her little mind games right now. They were here to get trashed—not to make feeble attempts at being deep and disturbing. She glanced at the clock. *Whoa.* It really *was* midnight. She couldn't quite believe it. Where had all the time gone? Maybe she was tipsier than she thought.

"Seven . . . six . . . five . . ."

Ariel stepped back into the shadowy living room. Jezebel and Jack were huddled around the TV, beers raised, counting along with a taped show of thousands of people who were actually having fun somewhere. Trevor stood off to the side, watching Jezebel. Poor Brian was still crashed on the floor. Ariel leaned forward to nudge him.

"Three . . . two . . ."

Then she froze.

"Jesus!" she whispered.

The living room curtains glowed with a reddish light—a light so bright that it made her squint. She stood up straight and blinked . . .

And then the light was gone.

Nobody said a word.

"Christ—what the hell was that?" Jack demanded after a moment.

It took Ariel a second to realize that the TV wasn't on anymore. Neither was the kitchen light. The low hum of the heater had stopped. She glanced around the room until her eyes came to rest on the only source of light she could find: a sliver of the moon, poking through a crack in the curtains.

"The power's out," Trevor said.

Ariel shook her head, then sighed. "Thanks, genius," she mumbled.

Well . . . whatever the flash was, it was over now. Except for the fact that they had no light, no heat, and no power.

Great. What a party.

Next year she would make *sure* to be somewhere else.

The Jump Club
New York City
3:01 a.m.

Julia Morrison breathed a long sigh of relief. For some reason the deafening music had abruptly stopped. The dance floor had been darkened. The only remaining light came from some glowing cigarettes and a few flickering red candles scattered about the room.

Maybe I can go home now, she thought sadly.

She was sleepy, and her ears were ringing. She never understood how people could stand to listen to such loud music for so long. It wasn't even real music; it was just a beat. She'd never gone for techno stuff—the repetitive *thump, thump, thump* that never changed. But who cared what she thought? Nobody. Least of all Luke. That much was obvious.

He was still dancing with that girl.

Couldn't he see that the party was over? The club owners had turned everything off—and Luke was still dancing. *Slow* dancing. Without music. By candlelight. He and the girl had their arms around each other, intertwined, like two snakes. Julia lowered her eyes. She couldn't look at them. She leaned back in the plush velvet couch and stared at the candle burning on one of the low tables nearby. She supposed

20

she could just curl up and go to sleep right here—

"Do you know what's going on?"

"Huh?" Julia glanced up. It was the guy sitting next to her, some slick man in a suit and a shirt buttoned all the way to the top. He looked confused.

"Do you know why they turned the music off?" he asked. "And the lights?"

Julia shrugged nervously. She didn't know what to say. The words might come out wrong, and she'd be exposed for what she was: a lonely and under-dressed seventeen-year-old girl who had no business being at a club at three in the morning. Then maybe she'd get kicked out. Which might not be a bad thing, except that Luke would lose his temper . . .

"Maybe it's last call?" she finally offered.

The man grinned at her. "Last call isn't until seven." He glanced around the darkened room, then stood up. "I bet DJ Snow is messing with our heads," he said, wandering off toward the bar. "DJ Snow pulled something like this last year, too. . . ."

Julia nodded, even though she had absolutely no idea what he was talking about. A bittersweet smile passed over her lips. Luke would probably sell his soul to trade places with that guy. He was every-thing Luke wanted to be: an insider at the Jump Club, good-looking, and probably loaded. She shook her head, staring at the candle.

Luke.

He'd been so cocky and proud when he scored those two fake IDs yesterday—like he'd finally become somebody important. Two one-way tickets to New York's best blowout. Free champagne at midnight and dancing till dawn. Who'd been there last year—some rapper? Someone famous. It was *the* place to be. Luke hadn't even bothered to ask Julia if she wanted to go. He'd busted his hump getting the IDs. So she didn't have a choice. He'd made that very clear.

It didn't matter that Julia hated dancing.

It didn't matter that Julia didn't drink.

It didn't matter that Julia dreaded New Year's Eve, *dreaded* it, because of that same December night three years ago . . . the way her mom and dad had waved good-bye . . . the phone call from the police and the ride to the morgue . . . the way she'd been forced to move to New York City to live with Uncle Clem . . . the way she'd lost everything to a drunk driver who was serving just four years in prison—*four years*—for vehicular manslaughter.

No. It didn't matter. Luke wanted to spend New Year's Eve *his* way. So he'd brought her here and dumped her on the couch. He'd discarded her like a broken toy while he chatted up some beautiful girl whose skin was so smooth and white that she could have starred in an Ivory soap commercial.

I'm not going to look at them, Julia promised herself. *I'm not going to give him the satisfaction of knowing how miserable I am.*

What had happened to her life anyway? What had she done to deserve to be so desperately lonely? If only she could trade places with somebody, a total stranger . . .

Wait a minute. She *was* a total stranger, wasn't she? In a way she was. Tonight she was a twenty-three-year-old somebody named Sharon Brown. She

22

dug into her jeans pocket and pulled out the fake ID. And when she squinted at the photo in the dim light, she almost managed to laugh. The girl didn't even look like her. Sure, they were both African American; they both had long brown curls—but that was as far as the resemblance went. Sharon Brown must have been at least thirty pounds heavier than Julia. Julia was skinny. Skin and Bones, her mom used to call her when Julia was a little girl.

"Put that away!" Luke's voice hissed.

Julia's head jerked up. She hadn't even heard him coming. His blue eyes were blazing. His pale skin seemed flushed in the orange glow of the candles.

Out of habit, her body tensed.

"What's wrong?" she asked.

He snatched the card out of her hands and shoved it into his back pocket. "Nobody just sits around and looks at their ID, you idiot," he growled. He glanced around the room. "Now it's obvious that it's fake. You're gonna get us both kicked out."

Julia bit her lip. Why was he so mad? Nobody was looking at them. But she was too frightened of him to raise her voice. And he knew it.

"What's your problem?" he demanded.

"Nothing," she mumbled wretchedly. She sighed and gazed around the dimly lit club. All the confident, stylish people were now shuffling in different directions, looking lost. The slick guy returned from the bar and sat back down next to her, absently slurping an exotic-looking drink. He stared into the crowd, clearly searching for a familiar face. It was almost funny in a way. Nobody knew what to do.

There was an undercurrent of bewilderment in the air. "I was just thinking that the place is probably closing now anyway," she added.

Luke shook his head, then flopped down on a nearby couch. "It's not. There's just some kind of problem with the power. A fuse blew or something."

Julia raised her eyebrows. "Are you sure?"

"Of course I'm sure," he stated. He frowned, then folded his arms across his chest. "Serena told me."

"Serena?"

He cast a quick, sidelong glance at her. "The girl I was dancing with."

"Oh, right." Julia swallowed. She forced a brittle smile. "Your new friend. What happened to her?"

"Jesus . . . don't start, Julia," he moaned. "It's not my fault that you don't like to dance."

Julia started grinding her teeth. *Just leave him!* the familiar voice silently screamed in the back of her head. *Right now! Just run out the door!* But she never listened to the voice. If she ran, he would find her. She could already envision the look in his eye, the tight fist raised above her face. And she couldn't fool herself: He was all she had. She had no friends in this city. Uncle Clem sure didn't give a damn about her. But where was the Luke she'd met all those months ago? The good-looking charmer? Had he even existed?

"It's cold in here," Luke suddenly complained. "You cold?"

Julia sighed. She hadn't noticed—but now that he mentioned it, she *was* a little chilly. There was a draft, as if somebody had opened all the doors.

The draft picked up a little.

She shivered, wrapping her arms around herself. Somebody *must* have opened the doors. She was going to say something—but a gust of winter wind swept through the room, swiftly extinguishing all the candles. The club was now pitch-black.

Julia drew in her breath.

"Oh, man," Luke grumbled. His disembodied voice seemed to float out from nowhere. Julia squirmed in her seat. People all around her started whispering heatedly. There was no reason to panic, none at all—but the whole thing was a little disturbing. New Year's Eve was bad enough without having to sit in the dark, in a strange place, surrounded by people she didn't know or *want* to know. How long did it take to change a fuse anyway?

"Julia?" Luke asked.

"Yeah?"

"You okay?"

Julia drummed her fingers on her knees. "Fine."

"Why don't you try to walk over and . . ." His voice began to fade—then fell to an incomprehensible mumble.

Julia pursed her lips.

"What did you say?" she asked.

If he answered, she didn't hear. There was a peculiar rushing noise in her ears. She shook her head.

"Luke?"

The noise grew louder. It sounded hollow—like wind rustling in the trees or the ripple of a distant waterfall . . . only there was a deep undertone, an ominous bass note hidden beneath it.

It wasn't coming from the club.

No. The sound was coming from somewhere else.

From *inside* her.

It was expanding, spreading through her body.

Julia clutched at the couch. Something was definitely wrong. She could barely feel the velvet. Her fingers were numb. She felt queasy, disoriented. Her insides were mushy, and her body was sagging, pushed downward, as if she were speeding blindly over the peak of a hill in a car that was going much too fast. . . .

Sunlight!

The darkness has lifted.

Yes, I can see the sun. It's high overhead, beating down on me . . . and it's hot, impossibly hot. The desert sun. I'm in the desert. There's nothing but dry, scorched earth, stretching all the way to the mountains. The sword is in my hand. I'm alone, but I have the sword. The Demon is near. I can hear its breath.

I have to face the Demon.

I force myself to stare into its eyes. They're black. Impossibly black. They glisten like two wet stones. The rest of its body is consumed in fire. I am afraid. But if I lift the sword and plunge it into the flames, I can—

"Julia!" Luke barked.

Her eyes popped open.

"What's wrong with you? We gotta get out of here! *Now!*"

"Wha-what do you mean?" she stuttered. It took her a moment to realize that she was sitting in the dark again. The nausea was gone. So was the rushing sound. In fact, the air was strangely quiet. She was still on the velvet couch . . . only Luke's voice was much closer. Had she fallen asleep? Or passed out? Had somebody slipped her some drugs? That hallucination or dream or whatever it was still clung to her—

"Julia, for Christ's sake!" Luke cried.

Julia swallowed. She couldn't get her bearings. "What's wrong?"

"The screaming," Luke whimpered. "The guy next to you . . . Serena . . . something happened to them."

Julia shook her head. She must be going crazy. Nothing was making any sense anymore.

"Touch that guy," Luke breathed. "Just touch him."

Julia reached blindly across the couch.

But the man was gone.

"*Touch* him!" Luke repeated.

Her fingers wiggled in the darkness. She was *trying* to touch the guy, but he wasn't there. Things were too weird. Somebody *must* have drugged her. That kind of sick prank happened all the time at parties like this, right? Her hand began to fall— slowly, slowly, until it dropped into something completely unexpected.

Something that felt like a steaming puddle of wet putty . . .

CHAPTER
THREE

University of Texas Hospital
Austin, Texas
2:07 a.m.

Dr. Harold Wurf was fed up.

New Year's Eve was *so* tedious. What with all the overdoses and drunk driving accidents, it seemed as if half the hicks in Austin needed their broken bones mended or their polluted stomachs pumped. Not that Harold did much mending or pumping, of course. He wasn't exactly a doctor—not yet. He was a resident. So legally he couldn't perform certain procedures.

True, he was the youngest resident at the hospital—and at the ripe age of twenty, the youngest person in history (yes, *history*) to graduate summa cum laude from the University of Texas Medical School. He *thought* of himself as a doctor. He *deserved* to be a doctor. And he certainly was a great deal more gifted than many of the doctors here.

But for now he could only run errands, draw blood, insert IV tubes . . . and observe the older people at work.

He was tired of observing.

At this point in the night he was just plain tired. He was also more than a little annoyed at having been assigned the grueling thirty-two-hour New Year's shift. He'd started at noon, and he wasn't even halfway through it.

What a crock, he thought. He strolled through the brightly lit, antiseptic hallway of the emergency ward, avoiding the stretchers that rolled past him and the doctors hurrying toward yet another catastrophe. Obviously he was well aware that he'd been assigned this shift because he was so brilliant and reliable. But didn't he deserve a break? His peers were out partying, or watching their kids, or getting laid—or whatever people in their late twenties did on New Year's Eve. But alas, he was *here.* He was a certified genius, for Christ's sake. There was no justice in this.

"Harold Wurf," a metallic voice announced over the loudspeaker. "Please report to the nurses' station immediately. Harold Wurf to the nurses' station."

Harold snorted. What now? Did somebody need a Band-Aid? If only some of the nurses were even *mildly* attractive, he wouldn't have dreaded the nurses' station so much . . .

Aha!

There was that patient in room 324, right at the end of the hall. He'd nearly forgotten about her. *She* was attractive. She was downright sexy. Yes. Long black hair, curvaceous body, about twenty-five years old—she very well might need some company. What was she here for . . . a concussion? Some sort of head wound. He picked up his pace. Yes, yes. The nurses would just have to wait for a moment. First he would work on his bedside manner.

He paused outside the woman's room. The

29

shade had been pulled over the window. He took a quick moment to study his reflection in the glass. Not bad. His wavy, longish brown hair framed his smooth jawline nicely; his ice blue eyes and broad smile were irresistible as always. No, not too shabby at all. It had been a good decision to let his hair grow these past few months. He straightened his white lab coat, then rapped on the door.

"Hello?" he said.

"Yes?" came the soft reply. "What is it?"

Harold grinned. Her voice was sexy, too—with just the perfect trace of a Texan accent.

"I'm Harold, one of the residents," he answered in deep, intimate tones. "I just wanted to check up on you."

There was a pause. Harold could hear the faint murmurings of a TV set.

"Um . . . okay," she replied after a moment. "But a nurse was just in here."

Harold pushed open the door and stepped into the room.

"It's always good to double-check vital signs in cases of head injury," he said reassuringly. He closed the door behind him.

Damn, he thought, giving her a quick once-over. She *was* gorgeous. She was propped up in bed in a skimpy little hospital gown, her large brown eyes glued to the TV on her night table. Her lips were full and red and parted just a little bit. Black hair cascaded from the thick white bandage around her head down past her shoulders.

"Have you been checking this out?" she asked.

30

"What's that?" He took her wrist and gently felt for her pulse. It was on the fast side—around 104 beats per minute. But she very well could be excited by *him,* too.

"The news," she said, gazing at the television. Her eyes had a dull, glazed appearance, but that might be due to her injury. "There's been one of those special reports. You know when they say, 'We interrupt your regularly scheduled programming'? It's totally freaky." She shook her head. "Wow."

Totally freaky? Harold repeated disdainfully to himself. So the woman wasn't going to be winning any Nobel Prizes. Of course, stupid women often made easier scores.

"What's freaky about it?" he asked with a friendly smile. His fingers lingered on her wrist.

"They're reporting all these blackouts everywhere. New York, Washington . . ." She reached for the remote control with her free hand and switched channels. "It's on every single station. It just happened, like, five minutes ago. They lost contact with the news desks in all these cities."

Harold nodded disinterestedly. Blackouts. Okay, yes, that was bizarre, fascinating, et cetera—but he had other things on his mind. He needed to distract her attention from the screen. He let his forefinger wander toward her palm, brushing the skin suggestively.

Her eyes drifted down to his hand.

Good, he thought. *That's much better. . . .*

"Easy there, Doogie Howser," she said with a snicker. She slid her wrist away from him and

31

pulled the covers over herself. "The nurses told me about you."

Harold frowned.

For the briefest instant he was consumed with rage at being humiliated by this ditzy fool. But then he forced the feeling aside. Losing self-control wasn't worth the effort. After all, he didn't want to risk his residency for a potential sexual harassment suit—over *this*. But judging from the way she was turning back to the TV with a wry smirk, it was clear that she didn't feel threatened. No, she probably thought of him as nothing more than an eager child. And that made him angry.

"My name's not Doogie Howser," he said after a moment.

She giggled. "Yeah . . . but don't you remember that show?" Her eyes remained pinned to the screen. "Come on, you *gotta* know about it. It was about a kid just like you. Some genius kid who became a doctor."

Harold flashed a phony smile. "It wasn't about a kid just like me," he said calmly. "It was about an ugly teenage nerd with bad acne. That isn't like me at all."

"So you *do* know it!" she exclaimed. She glanced at him—then burst out laughing.

Harold's smile faded. It was time to go to the nurses' station. If he stayed here any longer, he might say something he would regret. "Try to get some rest," he mumbled, turning his back on her. "Your pulse is elevated—"

"Wait," she commanded.

Uh-oh. She wasn't going to get him in trouble, was she? He glanced over his shoulder.

Her face seemed oddly flushed. She struggled to sit up straight.

"I . . . uh, I could use some water," she stammered. Her voice was hoarse, gravelly.

Harold peered at her closely. "Is something caught in your throat?"

She shook her head. "No, no, I'm hot," she choked out. All at once her face shriveled, as if she'd just caught a whiff of some powerfully foul odor. Tiny droplets of perspiration appeared on her nose. "I don't feel too good. . . ."

"Okay, just relax," he instructed, stepping swiftly back across the room. He shoved the last few minutes from his mind. The incident was over. Now he had a genuine crisis on his hands. He placed the back of his hand against her forehead. *Christ.* She was burning up. She twitched once. Her eyes rolled back in her head.

"Dammit," Harold muttered. He leaned over her and jabbed at the blue alarm button on the wall.

The woman started tearing at her gown. She might be having an epileptic fit. Harold held his breath, waiting for the code blue announcement over the intercom. Nothing happened.

"Come *on*," he growled. He punched the button again.

There was still no response. What the hell was going on?

Harold's eyes flashed back to the woman.

"Jesus," he said.

This was no seizure. It couldn't be. Evil-looking black welts were appearing over the entirety of her body. They spread with astonishing speed, like spilled ink. He'd never seen anything like this, never read about anything like it in any medical journal. His breath started coming fast. Why wasn't anybody responding to the code blue call? He reached forward to hit the alarm one last time—just as some of the welts burst. Blood and pus exploded in his face.

Terror consumed him instantly. He leaped back.

"Somebody help!" he shouted, staggering toward the door. He clawed at the hot, sticky liquid on his skin. "Somebody help!"

He threw open the door and stumbled out into the hall.

Then he stopped dead in his tracks.

The hall was deserted. Completely and utterly deserted. The doctors, nurses, patients, staffers, *everyone* . . . they had all vanished.

But for some unfathomable reason they'd also *stripped*—leaving their clothes abandoned in thick black puddles like discarded props on an empty stage.

FOUR

Route One, Outside of Jerusalem
Israel
11:10 a.m.

". . . still trying to determine the cause of the black-outs across the globe. Satellite imaging indicates that New York, London, Hong Kong, and Johannesburg are among the cities without power. . . ."

Sarah Levy leaned forward in the narrow seat of the rickety bus, straining to listen to the nasal British voice trickling out of the transistor radio on the dashboard. Luckily she and her granduncle happened to be sitting right behind the driver. But there was so much noise. The bus kept squeaking and bouncing, and the engine whined loudly as they climbed up the steep, twisting, dusty highway toward West Jerusalem. A few people had already huddled up front in the aisle to hear the news, their faces creased with worry.

The rest of the passengers were praying.

But Sarah wasn't worried. Not a bit. She'd never had much use for prayer either. She respected the religious beliefs of others, sure—but as far as she could tell after eighteen years on this planet, *God* was just a three-letter word for *imaginary friend*.

Her relatives, of course, did not share her views.

Her granduncle, Elijah, was praying, nodding back and forth beside her in the seat, eyes closed, his long white beard luminous in the morning sunlight. Even her little brother, Joshua, sitting across the aisle with his curly black hair sticking out from under his Yankees cap—even *his* lips were moving in silent prayer. His pale face seemed whiter than usual.

Sarah, on the other hand, was exhilarated. She'd never been around such big news—in the midst of it, *living* it. Excitement coursed through her veins. She might have been jittery about ten minutes ago, when the rocky landscape had glowed with that eerie red light—but she was fine now. Besides, the sky was a dazzling, cloudless blue. If they *were* in danger, if they were about to get bombarded with deadly cosmic rays or something, nobody on this bus could do anything about it. *Que será, será.* Whatever will be, will be. Prayer certainly wouldn't help.

". . . and scientists are surprised by the swiftness and brevity of the phenomenon," the announcer continued. "The prime minister has just issued an official statement from Tel Aviv, urging everyone to remain in their homes and stay calm until the experts have had a chance to gather more information. . . ."

"Baruch atah Adonai," Joshua was whispering anxiously in Hebrew. "Blessed art thou, O Lord, our God. . . ."

Poor kid, Sarah thought. She stole a quick peek at her fifteen-year-old brother. He was staring out the window, wringing his hands, his brown eyes shifting. But Josh had been a wreck ever since he'd arrived, even before the "phenomenon." He'd always been a little nervous, a little young for his age. He hadn't even wanted to *come* to Israel. It had been Mom and Dad's idea to force him to spend Christmas break with his big sister in Tel Aviv and his pious granduncle in Jerusalem.

Not exactly a barrel of laughs for a little kid like him.

A pang of guilt flashed through Sarah. The trip had been *her* idea, as a matter of fact. Mom and Dad had simply agreed to it. But she had a very good reason to bring him here: She wanted him to see their homeland. Members of the Levy family had been living in the Middle East for more than three thousand years. That was a pretty amazing fact in and of itself. And even if *she* wasn't spiritual or religious, Josh was. She figured she owed it to him to show him the country.

Deep down, of course, she just wanted a break from her studies. *And* to show her cute little brother off to all her brainy friends at the university.

A smile played on her lips. Josh would have fun sooner or later. At least it was sunny and sixty degrees here. It was three in the morning in New York and probably freezing—and according to the news, the city was in the midst of a blackout. She brushed a few strands of shoulder-length brown hair behind one ear and adjusted her wire-rimmed glasses. Now that she thought about it, Josh would probably be peeing in his pants if he'd stayed at home.

Elijah cleared his throat.

"Sarah, I have no more doubts that you'll make an excellent journalist," he murmured in his thick Israeli accent. "Not that I had any before, mind you."

"Why's that?" she asked, grinning.

Her granduncle's thoughtful black eyes sparkled. "Because you haven't uttered a peep," he replied. "You are the only one on this bus who is calm, detached, and collected. You're *smiling*. And I know the reason. You haven't heard all the facts yet. You're simply waiting. You are very practical that way. It's a gift."

Oh, please, Sarah thought. She shrugged embarrassedly. Elijah was always heaping praise on her. It wasn't that she had any special gift or anything. She just had an obsessive need to have everything *proved*. She hated guesswork. That was why she was an atheist. That was why she'd enrolled in a journalism program. And that was why she'd chosen the university in Tel Aviv over a regular four-year college back home in the States. Here in Israel, more than almost anyplace else in the world, truth and guesswork were *always* being confused for each other. She wanted to help set the record straight.

Of course, she'd also come here for the danger.

And the conflict. And the news that came out of it.

Maybe she was overly ambitious. But she firmly believed that the news—the simple act of *reporting the truth*—was the one thing in the world that could unite everyone, no matter what their ethnicity, religion, or creed. This bus was a perfect example. The mysterious red glow had turned the passengers into

38

a small family, drawn together by a common con-cern—from the small Arab child sitting behind her to the grizzled Orthodox Jew sitting next to Josh; from a gun-toting soldier to a Catholic nun. All of them were focused on the same thing: the need for truth. For these brief moments anyway, they were at peace with one another.

Sarah turned her attention back to the radio.

". . . Haifa? Yes, this just in from Haifa," the an-nouncer was saying. "Astronomers at the Haifa Observatory confirm what Jordanian, Egyptian, and other Israeli astronomers are describing as a massive solar flare. An anomaly on the sun's chromosphere . . ."

Elijah bolted upright in his seat. His eyes bulged.

"What's wrong?" Sarah asked, frowning.

"Solar flare," he whispered. "That's it. The first sign." He sounded absolutely terrified. He raised a trembling hand to his collar. "It was written: 'The sun reaches out and touches the earth.' Why didn't I think of it? It was written!"

Sarah stared at him, alarmed. He was babbling like a lunatic. "What was written?"

Elijah nodded to himself. His breath started coming in great, wheezy gasps. His whole body was trembling now—violently. Sarah swallowed. What was he talking about? Why was he so afraid?

"The scroll," he croaked. "You must find it . . . in the black box. . . ."

"What do you mean, Elijah?" she asked impa-tiently. She heard a pumping sound, then realized it was her own heart. "Start from the beginning."

Elijah clutched at his face. It was very red.

"What's wrong?" Josh pressed from the other side of the aisle.

Sarah shook her head. She had no idea what was wrong—only that her granduncle looked terrible: sweating and hyperventilating. She couldn't take her eyes off him. *The scroll?* "You must find it," Elijah repeated. "In my house. In the black box." The words were barely understandable. There was a gurgling noise in his throat, as if he were drowning. "I'm the only one who knows . . . you find it. I'm the only righteous man who knows. I should have told you earlier. The code is hidden in the scroll. Use the code." He shot her a crazed look. His face was soaking wet.

"*Find* it!" he hissed.

Sarah's heart was galloping now. Elijah was clearly ill. He *never* talked this way, like some kind of demented religious fanatic. They needed to stop the bus. Immediately.

"Elijah, just take it easy," she soothed—as much for herself as for her granduncle. "We'll get the driver to pull over." She reached out to touch her uncle's shoulder, to reassure him.

His jacket felt strangely warm.

She pushed the material harder. His clothing seemed to give a little, as if the flesh underneath the fabric wasn't solid. She stopped breathing. Something was pulsating unevenly under there . . . it didn't feel right. Her hand involuntarily flinched away from him.

"Unc-Uncle Elijah?" she stammered, unable to keep the fear out of her voice.

40

He didn't answer.

"Sarah?" Josh demanded, his voice rising. "Sarah, what is it? Oh, my God, *Sarah!*"

Sarah clamped her hands over her mouth. Her eyes widened. Elijah wasn't merely sick; he was *diseased*. His skin was splotchy. Horrid black blisters welled up on his cheeks. He scratched at his face, tearing the flesh. It came off in bloody chunks on his fingertips.

"Stop the bus!" Sarah screamed, leaping out of her seat. *"Stop it!"*

But nobody was behind the wheel.

Sarah gasped. Her eyes frantically darted to the floor.

No. It can't be . . .

Bile rose in her throat.

The bus driver had fallen in a limp, bloody heap next to his seat, only his body . . . his body seemed to be *melting,* turning to black liquid before her eyes. She blinked, then blinked again. How could this be happening? How could Elijah catch some awful flesh-eating disease at the exact same moment as this bus driver? Was *everybody* catching it?

Joshua!

She whirled to face her brother.

He gaped back at her, unspeaking, his skin as ghostly white as chalk.

But he was the only one left.

The rest of the passengers—the old Orthodox man, the Arab child, the soldier, the nun—all of them had collapsed, their bodies shifting, dripping, *changing. . . .*

"The bus!" Joshua cried. "The bus—"

Sarah's feet kicked up from underneath her. Her glasses flew off. Gravity hurtled her to the floor. Her head slammed into the dirty tile, and the next instant she was thrown against the bottom of one of the seats. Sharp metal tore into her back. But the pain was enough to cut through the shock.

The bus is out of control, she realized with cold clarity.

She rolled over on her stomach and began clawing her way toward the front. Panic fed her strength, pushing her inch by inch—right through the fetid liquid remains of the driver. The bus started swerving, teetering on one side. She lunged forward and threw her arms around the back of the driver's seat. She could plainly the see the huge wheel in front of her, spinning like a top, only inches away. But she couldn't grab it. If she grabbed it, she'd lose her balance. She *had* to sit.

With every ounce of strength she fought herself into the seat.

Too late.

The bus careened through the guardrail with a wrenching squeal—then off the road, plunging down a steep embankment toward a broken stone wall. Sarah squeezed her eyes shut. She slammed on the brakes. The bus jerked sluggishly. It slowed but didn't stop. She heard a shatter of glass, a high-pitched scream. . . .

And then, mercifully, the world faded to nothingness.

187 Puget Drive
Babylon, Washington
12:15 a.m.

Ariel drained the last of her beer and leaned back in the frayed easy chair. If she'd been bored to death fifteen minutes ago—well, then she'd already died and gone to boredom hell by now. Hardly anybody had said anything since the blackout. Of course, she was partly to blame. She *had* put a damper on the conversation. A mischievous smile crossed her lips. Everybody had taken her so goddamn seriously when she'd made that crack about having an orgy because it was the end of the world. It was just a harmless little joke. . . .

"Oh, my God," Jezebel suddenly whispered.

Ariel laughed. "Amen, sister. Say your prayers. Like I said, it's Judgment Day."

"Oh, my God," Jezebel repeated. She hopped up from the floor and began pacing around the room. "I just remembered something." Her voice rose. "This is . . . this is . . ."

"What?" Ariel demanded, furrowing her brow.

Jezebel stopped dead in her tracks and gazed at Ariel. "Don't you get it?" she cried. "You were right. This is what happens in a nuclear war. I saw this show once on the Discovery Channel. There's a bright flash and then the power goes out—"

"Please," Ariel moaned. "Jez, I was joking. Believe me, this is *not* a nuclear war. Don't you think we would have heard an explosion or something? It's already been, like, fifteen minutes."

"It depends," Trevor interjected. He sounded pleased with himself. "See, it depends on how far away the blast is." He strolled over to the window, parted the curtains, then peeked out on the street. "We may hear nothing. The speed of—"

"See?" Jezebel yelled, cutting him off. She ran toward the door. "I'm gonna try to start my car," she murmured. Her voice was quavering. She threw open the door so hard that it slammed against the wall. "If it's not working . . ." The words trailed into silence as she dashed outside.

Ariel laughed again. "Remind me never to bring *her* along in a crisis," she muttered.

"What's going on?" Brian's voice croaked from the floor.

"Hey—you're awake!" Ariel exclaimed happily.

"I am?" Brian groggily pushed himself into a sitting position and rubbed his eyes. "I don't *feel* like it. What was that noise?"

"Oh, nothing," Ariel replied. She took a sip of beer. "Jezebel decided she would freak out to pass the time. She's convinced the world's coming to an end."

"Shut the hell up, Ariel," Jack spat.

Ariel cocked an eyebrow at him. "Hey, Jackie boy?" she replied calmly. "It's not my fault that your girlfriend is a . . . what's that word you love? Oh, yeah: a *wuss*. Oh—and Jack, honey, would you mind closing the front door? It's getting cold in here."

Jack didn't budge.

Brian shook his head, clearly disoriented. His puffy eyes wandered from Trevor to Ariel to Jack to the open door. "I'm sorry," he mumbled. "I think I'm still a little buzzed. *What's* going on?"

"Possibly a nuclear war," Trevor replied, still peering out the window.

Ariel opened her mouth—but unfortunately Jezebel sprinted back through the door before she could manage an appropriate obscenity.

"My car won't start," Jezebel panted, her face twisted with fear. "It's dead."

Hmmm. Dead? Much to Ariel's surprise, a nervous twitter passed through her stomach. *Should* they be freaking out? No. Of course not. There must be a perfectly logical explanation. . . .

Oh, crap.

Somebody else was walking up the front steps.

Okay, *now* they should be freaking out. Ariel knew the deliberate stomp of those heavy shoes all too well. Judging by the way everyone started staring at the carpet, they *all* knew that stomp. The stomp belonged to her father—that being one Stephen Collins, the man who was built like a professional TV wrestler and had the loony temper to match. But what on earth was he doing home? He should still be at their neighbors' house, the Wallaces. He said he wouldn't be back until two at the earliest. . . .

Mr. Collins strode through the door in his scarf and overcoat. His fat belly hung over his baggy pants. He took one long look around the room, then shook his head in disgust.

Uh-oh. Even when her dad *wasn't* angry, he was pretty intimidating.

"What the hell is going on in here?" he snapped, looking directly at Ariel. "I thought you were going out. Where did you get all this beer?"

Ariel began to feel ill. She'd already forgotten about the flash, or the nuclear war, or *whatever* it was. Trevor was right: Her dad *was* going to kill her. Now that she thought about it, a nuclear war might actually be preferable to this.

Her father's beady green eyes bored into Ariel's own. "Young lady, I'm asking you a question. None of you are legal yet. I *know* Brian doesn't turn twenty-one until June, and I certainly—"

"Mr. Collins?" Jezebel interrupted in a panicked, high-pitched voice. "Listen, I'm sorry about all the alcohol, but did you see that flash? Like fifteen minutes ago?"

Ariel lowered her eyes. For a split second she almost felt like laughing. Good old Jez. Ariel could always count on her best friend to bail them out of a touchy situation.

"What does *that* have to do with anything?" Mr. Collins barked.

"It . . . um, it doesn't," Jezebel stammered. "But do you have any idea what it was?"

"Some kind of power outage or something," he

grumbled. "That's why I left the Wallaces'. But what I want to know is . . ." He let the sentence hang.

Ariel glanced up.

Her father wasn't looking at anyone anymore. He wasn't talking. He was staring at his own hands, eyes wide. Even in the pale light of the moon Ariel could see that his forehead was suddenly dripping with sweat.

"Dad?" she asked nervously.

He looked at her—then collapsed.

"Dad!" Ariel shrieked.

She leaped out of the chair. He was writhing on the floor, his body crumpled in a fetal position. But he didn't make a sound. *Heart attack* was all she could think. She fell to her knees by his side. What were you supposed to do in case of a heart attack? She'd seen *ER* enough times. He couldn't be having a heart attack, though; he wasn't *that* fat. Had he smoked some bad pot or something at the Wallaces'? This couldn't be happening. . . .

Ariel buried her face in her hands.

Okay, I'm dreaming, she told herself desperately. *I've had too much to drink. When I open my eyes, I'll wake up in bed.*

The room fell dead quiet.

Ariel took a deep breath. She decided to count to ten. Slowly. Then she would look. Maybe her father was okay now. After all, nobody was crying or anything, right?

One . . . two . . .

Yeah. This was all right. It felt good to count. It

47

was like feeling her way into the future, step by step. Maybe her father was playing a practical joke. Her thoughts began to wander back to a long forgotten memory. She and her father were playing catch. He suddenly keeled over. Boom. Right into the grass. Ariel came running, terrified. But then he swooped her up in his arms, laughing hysterically. . . .

Nine . . . ten.

It was over.

Everything was going to be okay.

Ariel let her hands drop.

A part of her truly expected to see the morning sunlight streaming through her bedroom window. Or her father, looking up at her and grinning with that wild-eyed grin.

But she didn't see either.

All she saw were her father's overcoat, scarf, shirt, and shoes—lying in a puddle of black goo on the floor.

PART II

January 2–January 16, 1999

CHAPTER SIX

Route One, Outside of Jerusalem
Israel
Morning of January 2

"Sarah?"

It was a whisper—faint and distant, from some other universe.

"Come on, Sarah."

The whisper grew louder.

"That's it! Wake up! I know you can do it."

Josh, Sarah realized. But where was he? She was aware of only darkness, a fuzzy invisible blanket separating her from her brother.

"Come *on,* Sarah," he pleaded.

Slowly, gradually, she became aware of something else. *Pain.* Her back and her face ached terribly. The pain floated up through the foggy layers of her consciousness . . . growing more and more acute until she groaned. She was stretched out on her back, lying on something soft and uneven. But why was she hurting so badly? She tried to lick her lips. Her tongue wouldn't move. It was bone-dry.

"Sarah, can you hear me?" Josh asked. His voice was right above her.

Yes, she thought—but no words would come. She forced a nod. "Can you open your eyes?"

Open my eyes? She hadn't even realized they were closed. Her eyelids fluttered. A formless white light assaulted her pupils. She blinked and squinted. . . .

Finally she made out the blurry shape of her brother's head, floating in space above her against a blue background.

Josh sighed deeply. "Thank God," he whispered.

Sarah tried to swallow. Her thirst was overwhelming. Summoning all of her feeble energy, she gasped: "Water."

Josh nodded. His head vanished from sight, then abruptly reappeared. He brought something small and red close to her mouth.

"It's not water; it's Coke," he said. "I'm sorry. I tried to save water, but I—uh, I ran out." He sounded ashamed.

Ran out? she wondered. The words struck her as strange, even though she wasn't sure why. She puckered her lips. Josh tilted the can. The syrupy liquid splashed on her tongue. It was warm and flat—but Coke had never tasted so good. She started gulping furiously.

"Careful," Josh warned, pulling the can away.

Some of the soda dribbled down her cheeks.

"You don't want to choke," he added. "You're probably dehydrated."

Sarah's eyes narrowed. "Why?" she murmured.

Josh hesitated. "You don't remember . . . the crash?"

The crash!

A flood of nightmarish images whirled through her mind: Elijah's diseased face, the melting bus

51

driver, the stone wall . . . then blackness. It was as if a dam had broken. Her throat tightened. She felt dizzy. Her stomach convulsed—and for a moment she was certain she would vomit. She squirmed, struggling to prop herself up on her elbows.

"Don't try to move," Josh instructed.

Sarah collapsed down on her back. Even if she'd wanted to move, she couldn't. The sudden memory drained her completely.

"Rest for a minute," he said. "I'm gonna give you your glasses in a sec. I found them this morning. They didn't even break. Can you believe that? I thought last night they were gone for sure."

"Last night?" Sarah croaked. Fortunately the nausea subsided. But it left a dull hunger in its place. She shook her head. "What do you mean?"

Josh didn't answer right away. He took a deep breath, then delicately slipped her glasses onto her nose. His small, pale face came into crisp focus.

Oh, my . . . Sarah couldn't believe how bad he looked. His forehead was bruised, his lip was cut, and his cheeks were drawn and haggard. He was kneeling beside her in the shadow of some enormous, twisted hulk of white metal. *The bus,* she realized with a shudder. She could barely recognize it.

"You've been unconscious for nearly twenty-four hours," Josh stated.

"What?" she cried.

Josh nodded somberly.

Sarah's mouth hung open—then snapped shut, seemingly of its own will. She was flabbergasted. Twenty-four hours? How was that possible? She quickly surveyed her surroundings. The wrecked bus lay wrapped around an old stone wall at the bottom of a barren, rocky hill. A *steep* hill. Dark tire tracks rose from the site of the crash—up, up, up to a twisted gap in the guardrail maybe a hundred yards above them. The ruined metal gleamed in the sun against the blue sky. She winced.

Now she understood. She was lucky to be alive.

"See, you flew right out the windshield and landed in the grass on the other side of the fence," Josh continued, as if she'd asked him a question. His voice was strange. He sounded very dry, very matter-of-fact—not at all like himself. "So it was a soft fall. You got a few cuts and scratches, but I don't think you broke anything. I dragged you over here to get you out of the sun. Then I spread you out on some clothes. And then, um . . . then I just waited. Right here. And I prayed."

A sickening thought suddenly occurred to her.

"You spent the *night* here?" she asked.

Joshua shrugged and lowered his eyes. "It wasn't so bad," he murmured. "I . . . I found enough clothes to keep me warm. And there was plenty, you know—plenty of food." He seemed to stumble awkwardly over the words.

Sarah stared at him. He was wearing his Yankees cap pulled low, but he was huddled in an oversized long black coat that she'd never seen before. She chewed her cracked lower lip. *Plenty of food*. They hadn't packed any food for themselves. The ride from Tel Aviv was only about an hour. Her eyes wandered to the ground. It was strewn with used sandwich wrappers, a couple of empty bottles, and some odd bits of dusty clothing. She looked back at Josh.

He returned her gaze—silent and stone-faced.

Oh, God.

Josh must have scrounged for food and clothing among the dead passengers.

"Are we the only . . . ?" She couldn't finish the question. He nodded. "They're all gone. Everyone on the bus. They just disappeared."

"Disa . . . disappeared?" she repeated. Once again her eyes fell to the abandoned clothes.

All those people were dead. Not just dead. *Gone.* Including her granduncle.

That meant while she'd been unconscious, Josh had been alone. Cold, hungry, and alone. Instead of trying to climb to the highway and look for help, he'd stayed by his sister's side all night. Down here—in this pit. In the middle of nowhere.

A hard lump formed in Sarah's throat. Despite the aches in her back she forced herself to sit up straight. "Come here," she breathed hoarsely.

Josh's lips quivered.

He hesitated, then fell into her arms. His entire body was shaking.

"I'm so sorry," she murmured, squeezing her eyes shut. "I'm so sorry, Josh."

Josh began to cry. "This isn't the way it's supposed to be," he sobbed quietly.

Sarah wrapped herself around him as tightly as she could. The plaintive sound of his voice stabbed into her body—far worse than any physical pain she felt. Josh should never have come here. He should have stayed at home with Mom and Dad, safe and sound. . . .

"It's supposed to be different," he wept.

"I know, I know," she whispered, gently stroking his hair. A tear fell from her cheek. "We'll be all right, though. We'll make it."

"No, no." He sniffed. "I mean, it isn't supposed to happen like *this*."

She drew apart from him. "What isn't, Josh?"

He rubbed his eyes, then shot her a penetrating stare. "The end of the world. Judgment Day."

She paused. "What?"

"You heard me," he said. The look in his eyes was very similar to the look Elijah had before the bus went off the road—haunted and unbalanced.

Oh, no. Please, no. Sarah began to feel sick again. Josh couldn't afford to waste time with this apocalyptic nonsense *now*—not when they needed to pull themselves together, get up to the highway, and find some help.

"Look, Josh," she began, as quietly and calmly as she could. "I know you've just been through hell. You experienced a lot of really traumatic, really horrible stuff. But that's *all* it was. It has nothing to do with Judgment Day. See, there was something bad on that bus. Whatever it was made all those people die—"

"Sarah, don't you get it?" he wailed. He jumped up and thrust his arms toward the sky. "There's something bad *all around us!*" He spun, the long

55

sleeves of his newfound black coat flopping list-lessly over his head. "And Uncle Elijah knew it. I've been thinking about it all night."

Sarah's head drooped. She couldn't argue; she didn't have the strength.

"It started with that thing with the sun," Josh stated. He kicked at the dust. "The solar flare. Elijah said that was the first sign. How do you explain that?"

Sarah raised her head. *The solar flare.* She'd been so consumed with the crash that she'd forgotten all about *that* part of it: the strange glow, the news reports of blackouts . . . right before everybody started collapsing. Her eyes narrowed. Was there a connection between the deaths and the flare? There *must* be.

"See?" Josh yelled. "See? Elijah knew it was the first sign."

Sarah frowned. She needed to put an end to this conversation—immediately. "Josh, even if the flare somehow killed the people on the bus, it has *nothing* to do with Judgment Day. Okay?" Her voice was flat. "We need to concentrate on more important things right now, like getting out of here."

Josh glared at her. "How do *you* know it's not Judgment Day?" he asked. "Huh? Can you prove that it isn't?"

Sarah sighed miserably. "Look, Josh, I . . . I—don't know," she stammered. "I mean, isn't there supposed to be fire and brimstone and stuff like that? Isn't—"

"The solar flare was written somewhere," he interrupted. "Like Elijah said. He believed in it."

"Yeah, well, why is Elijah dead, then?" Sarah cried. "You'd think if he believed in Judgment Day, *he* would have survived it, right?" Her voice cracked, then fell to a hoarse whisper. She was too weak to shout. "Isn't that how it works? Aren't the good people supposed to inherit the earth or something?"

Josh shook his head. "Do we really know how good Elijah was?" he asked. "Think about it. Everybody has secrets, Sarah. Everybody. And only God knows what they are."

Sarah stared at him. She almost laughed. She couldn't believe what she was hearing. Her brother really *was* going nuts. "So you're saying that Elijah was some kind of closet sinner? Josh—do you know how *ridiculous* that sounds? He prayed every single day! He freaked out if I ate hot dogs that weren't kosher! Believe me, whatever secrets he had, I'm sure *mine* are a lot worse."

Josh didn't say anything. He just kept shaking his head.

"I mean, don't you think it's a little weird that *I'm* alive and he's dead?" she demanded. "*I'm* the one who doesn't believe in any of that garbage, and—"

"Enough already," Josh cut in. His tone was harsh, final. He turned and glanced up the hill to the highway. "We can't waste time fighting like this. We need to get to his apartment and find that scroll or black box or whatever he was talking about."

"I agree we should stop fighting," Sarah said. "But I think we should flag down a car and go to a hospital and get checked out by a doctor. Then we should call Mom and Dad."

Josh whirled to face her. "What makes you think there's even gonna *be* a hospital?"

Sarah moaned, then lay back down on the pile of clothes. "Josh, you're not making any sense," she mumbled dully. "Why wouldn't there be a hospital?"

"Maybe because the world is falling apart," he stated. "I hate to tell you this, Sarah, but I've been sitting down here in this hellhole for twenty-four hours, and nobody has stopped to help us—or even *look*. Last night all these kids were running down the highway, screaming and crying and I don't even know what. I yelled to them, but nobody stopped. This morning I heard tons of cars going by and *still* nobody stopped. Don't you think that's weird?"

Sarah returned his gaze, but her heartbeat jumped. *Nobody stopped.* Wouldn't people want to help them? Unless . . .

She stared blankly into space. The pain in her back suddenly seemed far away. What if *lots* of people died? She'd just assumed that the people on the bus were the only ones who had gotten sick. But why? She had no proof. And neither did Josh—not after twenty-four hours. A whole entire *day.* The skin on the back of her neck began to crawl. She sat up straight. No, it would be a whole lot *more* weird if the people on the bus *were* the only ones who died.

After all, the flare had affected all those cities around the globe—the ones that were hit with blackouts. Including New York. *Oh, Jesus.* Mom and Dad . . .

"See what I mean?" Josh asked quietly.

Sarah nodded. She was unable to speak.

"Listen, we'll try to get to a hospital," Josh said. His tone softened. "I promise. But if we can't—for whatever reason—then we go to Elijah's house. Deal?"

Sarah looked at him. "Deal."

Something struck her then: For the first time in their lives, Josh was taking charge of the situation. *He* was telling *her* what to do. And she was very, very relieved. Because at that moment she was far too weak and terrified to make any kind of decision for anybody—least of all herself.

SEVEN

Pittsburgh City Jail
Pittsburgh, Pennsylvania
Afternoon of January 3

"What the hell are you *lookin'* at, George?"

George Porter's grip tightened around the cold metal gate of the holding pen. His knuckles turned white. He wasn't going to answer Eight Ball's idiotic questions. He wasn't going to *look* at Eight Ball. If he looked at Eight Ball one more time, he would kill the son of a bitch.

Anyway, he couldn't stop himself. The water cooler was so close. He'd been staring at it for hours now. It was right on the other side of the wire mesh. Right beyond his reach. Right next to the pile of the dead cop's clothes, next to the dead cop's desk. So freaking close . . .

"Stop *looking!*" Eight Ball shouted. "You're pissin' me off."

"Shut up," George growled. He ran a shaky hand through his stringy platinum blond hair. The dye was starting to come off. His sweaty palms were turning a sickly yellow.

"I'm tellin' you—lookin' at that water is only gonna make you thirstier," Eight Ball said. "Give it up already."

That's it. George whirled to face him. Then he grimaced. *Blecch.*

He hadn't noticed earlier, but starving to death in a cell wasn't doing much to improve Eight Ball's looks. That was for damn sure. The kid's fat, pale face was slowly turning the same creamy color as the inside of a Twinkie . . . except for the bags under his eyes and a few new zits. His gray T-shirt was smeared with the chocolate they'd eaten three days ago—the last thing either of them had put in their mouths. He looked like a goddamn pig. Yup. Especially the way he was sitting right next to a puddle of his own piss. He hadn't even had the decency to pee outside the bars. It was starting to seriously reek in here.

"What are you lookin' at?" Eight Ball demanded.

"Not much," George grumbled. "I just never realized how butt-ugly you were."

Eight Ball chuckled. "You ain't exactly Brad Pitt, my man. Look at you. You're a little twerp. I always meant to ask you, are those fake contacts or what? Nobody has ugly-ass green eyes like that. You look like a mix between a bucket of puke and that loser from—"

"Shut up!" George shouted. He blinked a few times and swallowed hard. He had to get out of here. Eight Ball was pushing him over the edge. He would die if he were trapped in this stinking cell any longer. He knew it. Hunger was eating his stomach alive. He was already losing his mind. Those weird, trippy flashes he kept having . . .

"*Make* me shut up," Eight Ball spat.

George's lips twitched. "I just might," he hissed.

"You know, if it wasn't for you, I wouldn't even *be* here."

"Gimme a break," Eight Ball moaned. "Hot-wiring that car was *your* idea, you idiot."

"Yeah, but *you* were stupid enough to get us caught." George glared at Eight Ball, shifting from side to side in his heavy black Dr. Martens. He'd never wanted to bash in somebody's brains as badly as he did at that moment. "I shouldn't even *be* in jail," he muttered, half to himself. "They shouldn't have locked me down. I'm not even an adult."

Eight Ball sneered. "In the eyes of the law sixteen *is* an adult, dummy."

"*What* law?" George snarled. He thrust a finger at the rumpled uniform outside the pen. "The law's gone, fat boy. Remember? The law is a guy who turned into a pile of greasy black slop right in front of your face. And he took the keys to this cell with him."

Eight Ball didn't say anything. He stared back at George, then sucked in his breath. "You know, I been thinking," he murmured quietly.

"Yeah, well—there's a first time for everything," George mumbled.

"No, *listen,* man." His voice grew sharp. "I'm serious. What if we're already dead?"

George scowled at him. *"What?"*

"I mean it. Like, what if this is hell or something?" He lowered his eyes and began picking at his dirty fingernails. "What if we died on New Year's Eve? How else would you explain it? We're stuck in this holding pen with no way out. The keys are just out of our reach. We can see that water. That's what hell is supposed to be like: You can *see* stuff, but you can't get to it. How else would you explain the way those cops just, like . . . *dissolved* like that?" His lips pressed into a tight line. "They locked us up, then they dissolved. You think this is bad now? It's only been three days. Just wait. We're stuck here forever, just the two of us. . . ."

Oh, brother. George rolled his eyes and turned his attention back to the cooler. So Eight Ball was going crazy, too. Why couldn't the fat prick just jabber to himself instead of out loud? Did he really think he was dead? Personally, George was too damn hungry to be dead. No . . . this wasn't hell. No way. George didn't know *what* it was—or what it was that killed those cops. He didn't really want to think about it either. It just reminded him of his rotten luck. Yup. Chances were that he was going to die in jail, with this moron by his side.

". . . you *listening* to me?" Eight Ball was asking.

George laughed harshly. "What's the point?"

"Look at me when I'm talking to you," Eight Ball snapped.

George sighed and turned his head.

Jesus. Now that he thought about it, Eight Ball really *did* look like a chubby little pig, sitting there in his own filth.

Hmmm.

If he *looked* like a pig . . . would he taste like one, too?

Maybe. He would definitely make a hell of a

meal. Hadn't George seen a movie once about a bunch of kids in a plane crash who ended up eating each other? Yeah. It was called *Alive*. His foster parents had rented it. The survivors of the crash ate their dead buddies. They lived a pretty long time, too . . . like two months. The movie sucked. But hey, it was based on a true story. The survivors wound up being heroes, if he remembered right. So cannibalism wasn't *all* bad. He almost grinned. Maybe he should just kill Eight Ball and get it over with.

"What?" Eight Ball asked. His voice was gruff. "Why are you looking at me like that?"

"No reason," George replied innocently.

For a moment Eight Ball's face swam in and out of focus.

Whoa.

George swayed on his feet—then grabbed the gate to steady himself.

"What's wrong with you?" Eight Ball demanded.

He shook his head, frowning. There was a ringing in his ears. He felt as if he'd just sniffed glue or something. *Uh-oh.* No, this was much more powerful than any cheap buzz. He knew this feeling. He'd felt this way yesterday, too, right before—

The ocean.

I can see it far below me.

I see the waves in the night—crashing against the rocks. I'm holding on to the baby. My baby. But why am I on the cliff? I can't let her fall. The moon is pulling her . . . out of my hands, with a grip so strong I can't possibly fight it.

64

My baby!

It's too late. She's tumbling down, down, into the sea. And if she dies, the Demon—

George whirled and slammed his fist into the cinder block wall. Pain shot through his arm, all the way up to his shoulder—but the vision abruptly died.

He was back in the pen.

Eight Ball was pushing himself to his feet. His face was etched with fear. His blubbery body was quivering like a bowl of Jell-O.

"George?" he whispered.

Gotta get out, George thought, panting. The crazy hallucination was too much for him to handle. His eyes darted wildly around the room. Nothing. The only way out was to break through the wire gate. But if that was what he would have to do, he would do it. The gate wasn't all *that* thick. Without another moment's hesitation he hurled himself across the floor—then leaped into the air, kicking his feet up and flying into the mesh like a baseball player sliding into home plate.

"Aah!"

There was a sharp *crack* in his right foot—followed instantly by the most horrible, excruciating pain he'd ever experienced.

The gate rattled violently.

The next thing George knew, he was rolling on the floor, his eyes squeezed tightly shut.

"My foot!" he gasped in agony. "My foot—"

"Hey, you knocked one of the screws loose!" Eight Ball cried.

George's eyelids popped open. One of the screws? Who *gave* a crap? He'd just broken his foot, for Christ's sake.

But Eight Ball didn't seem to care. He was grinning. He scurried over to the gate and crouched beside George, then began viciously tugging at a screw near the bottom of the thick iron frame that held the gate in place.

George groaned. It didn't *look* very loose.

"If I can get this one out, I can punch through," Eight Ball muttered. "Don't you remember? I punched through that air-conditioning vent in the girls' bathroom once."

Girls' bathroom . . . George stared at Eight Ball from the cold cement floor, not believing his eyes or ears. But the fool kept yanking at that screw, twisting it in his chubby fingers. He must really think he could get it out. He grunted with the effort. His tongue poked out the side of his mouth. His face grew redder and redder. . . .

It popped free.

Eight Ball beamed triumphantly. He tossed the screw over his shoulder, then peeled his T-shirt off his body and wrapped it around his hand. Rolls of white flesh jiggled as he moved. He drew back his arm and slammed his shirt-covered fist into the bottom of the gate with a loud *thwack*.

Once again the metal rattled loudly.

The wire grid seemed to give a little. There was a little space between the edge of the gate and the frame.

"I'll be damned," George whispered.

Eight Ball began punching furiously—again and again, putting all two-hundred-odd pounds of his weight behind each blow.

The space widened.

George shook his head. In spite of the pain he almost chuckled. Eight Ball was doing it. He was really doing it. . . .

Finally Eight Ball stopped. His body was moist with sweat. He took a deep breath, then forced his head through the space, squirming and kicking and pushing. The rest of his body began to squeeze through the hole. George cringed. Jagged wire sliced into Eight Ball's stomach, but he didn't stop. He groaned and shimmied—then with one last huge grunt he forced the widest part of his scratched belly through the gate. Blood dripped onto the floor. A moment later legs slithered after him.

He was out.

"You did it!" George cried.

Eight Ball laughed, then spun around on his hands and knees to face him. "What did I tell you?" he gasped. His breath stank like a sewer, but George didn't mind. Nope. Everything was just fine.

"Careful when you're pulling me through," George instructed. "I . . ." He paused.

A wicked smile had appeared on Eight Ball's face.

George swallowed. "What's wrong?"

"I ain't pullin' you through," he replied simply.

"What?"

Eight Ball laughed again, then pushed himself to

his feet. "I need to eat first. And get some smokes."

No, George thought, growing cold. *No . . .*

Eight Ball turned and shuffled out the door. "See ya later, Georgie boy!" he called.

"Get back here!" George shrieked. He tried to move but wound up flopping over on his back. What was he thinking? He couldn't stand. His freaking foot was broken. It would never support him. "Come back!" he pleaded desperately. "I'm sorry! Come on, man!"

But Eight Ball's footsteps faded.

I don't believe it. That fat piece of crap.

He was gone.

And he wasn't coming back either. George would bet his life on it. He had no choice *but* to bet his life on it. His life was all he had left.

Unless he really *was* in hell.

Funny. That notion didn't seem so far-fetched anymore.

EIGHT

675 East 110th Street, Apartment 1401
New York City
Morning of January 6

1/6/99

I just had another vision. Thank God
Luke isn't here. That makes eight since
New Year's Eve. This one was different,
though. I still saw myself stabbing the
demon, but when I woke up, I knew I
had to get out of New York City. It
was weird. It was like, wham: Time to
leave. I don't know how I knew. I just
did. The answer to this thing, whatever
it might be, isn't here. And if I don't
try to find the answer, something
bad's going to happen. Not just to me.
To all of us, all the people who are
left. I'm sure of it.

On the other hand, I might be going
crazy. That's a major possibility. It's
just one that I don't like thinking about.

I have to ask myself, How much worse can things get? Every day when I look out the window, I see something sick. Every single day. I thank the Lord that Uncle Clem lives on the fourteenth floor. Nobody's bothered to come up here yet. There's still no electricity, so the elevator doesn't work. I guess rapists and looters are too lazy to climb all those stairs. Yesterday I saw a skinhead split some girl's skull open with a bat. Just like that. Right outside. It was like watching a horror movie from really far away. She's still out there, lying in the snow.

The really scary thing is, I didn't even _think_ about trying to help her.

I haven't left Uncle Clem's apartment. Not once. I'm too afraid. Every time Luke goes out, he comes back with a story about how he almost got shot or beat up. He's had to fight for food in abandoned stores. He's had a black eye for three days now. He says that there are all kinds of rumors on the street about what happened. Either Iraq dropped some kind of biological bomb on us, or God is punishing the human race for being so screwed up, or it's an alien invasion but the aliens are invisible . . . blah, blah, blah. For all I know, Luke might have made up all those rumors himself. With no news, no TV, no radio, and no contact with the rest of the outside world, it's anybody's guess why millions of people suddenly turned into black slime and disappeared.

Me, I don't know _what_ happened on New Year's Eve. But I know this: Whatever it was, it has something to do with these visions I'm having. I'm sure of it. I'm more sure of it than anything in my whole entire life.

Now all I have to do is tell Luke.

Ha! It looks so easy on paper. I'd almost rather trade places with that girl outside than tell him about it. Okay, that's not true. But I know he's going to get freaked, and mad, and all that. Still, I have to speak up. I can't lie anymore. Every time it happens, I just say that I had a dizzy spell or that I fainted or something. He's not going to buy it much longer. I _have_ to get out. Besides, there's

71

nothing for me here. This place is a dump.
We finished all the food. There's no
water. Uncle Clem is gone. Luke's parents
are gone. Everybody I know is

Julia stopped writing. She lifted her pencil. Something was rustling in the hall outside the front door.

"Luke?" she asked nervously. She could see her breath, a cloud of white vapor in the stark, squalid living room.

"Yeah, it's me. Open up."

As quietly as she could, she closed her tattered diary and shoved it deep inside her coat pocket. The diary was a secret. Her words, her *thoughts*—those were hers. Luke could never know of them or invade them. She hopped up from the moth-eaten orange couch.

Brrrr, she said to herself.

She shivered. Was it colder today than it had been for the past few days? It must be. Her toes were numb.

"Hurry up," his muffled voice ordered. "I'm tired."

"Coming." She ran across the cracked linoleum to the front door, then fumbled as fast as she could with the dead bolt, the chain, and the lock. "Sorry," she apologized. "I was on the couch, and—"

Luke kicked open the door and wordlessly brushed passed her. Julia followed him with her eyes. Her shoulders sagged.

Oh, Luke.

He was cradling a half-empty bottle of whiskey in his gloved hands. That was all. He slumped into the couch without looking at her. His nose was bright red—but whether that was from the cold or the whiskey, she had no idea. A few brown crumbs clung to the side of his mouth. He must have eaten a brownie or Ho Hos or something.

Neither of them spoke for a few moments.

In the silence Julia's stomach growled.

"I thought you were going to get some food," she said quietly.

He shrugged, then leaned back in the couch and took a leisurely sip from the bottle.

Julia chewed on the inside of her cheek. Soft rage was welling up within her. She folded her arms in front of her chest. "Luke?"

His Adam's apple rose and fell rapidly several times. Finally he pulled the bottle from his lips and took a deep breath. "I looked for food," he mumbled. "The store was cleaned out. The shelves were empty. There was nothing."

Liar! she thought. *You liar!*

"What?" he asked defensively. "I told you, the store was cleaned out—"

"So you got some booze instead," she interrupted, unable to stop herself. She was going to comment on the crumbs, but she closed her mouth at the last moment. She knew better than to push too far.

His deep blue eyes darkened. "You got a problem with that?"

"Don't *you?*" she cried. "It's early in the morning, Luke! The sun just came up, like, two hours ago!"

He laughed, then raised the bottle and swished the whiskey inside. Now his eyes were glittering maniacally, as if he were a mental patient. "What can I say, baby? Scotch is the breakfast of champions."

You're sick. She shook her head. But what did she expect? It was typical. He'd helped himself to a snack, then headed straight for the abandoned liquor store. It probably never even crossed his mind that *she* hadn't eaten since yesterday afternoon. She stared at her sneakers. She couldn't stand the sight of him anymore.

"So what did you do up here while I was out anyway?" he asked.

"Nothing," she lied.

"Yeah, right. I bet you were writing all your secrets in that little diary of yours."

Her head jerked up.

"That's right." He smirked. "I found it in your coat. Pretty interesting stuff, Julia."

Her eyes widened. Cold dread gripped her body like a vise. She trembled involuntarily. *Oh, God, no* . . .

"Mm-hmm. I read it this morning while you were asleep." He laughed once. His nostrils flared. "I gotta hand it to you, Jules. I mean, I used to think you were selfish and underhanded, but this . . . this takes the cake. I go out there every single day and risk my life looking for food for *you*"—he thrust the bottle toward her—"and you sit up here in this apartment, all safe and warm, calling me a jerk behind my back. Now how do you think that makes me feel? Huh? I'm curious."

"Luke, you—it's not . . . it's not what it seems,"

she stuttered. She began backing toward the door. "Nothing in there is . . . I mean, I don't *mean* what I write, like, literally or anything." The words poured out of her mouth in a whispery, nonsensical jumble. But she knew there was no hope. Nothing she could say would prevent a beating. Nothing. "Luke, please, you—"

"And what's up with these *'visions'* you've been having?" he interrupted. He made little quotation marks in the air with his fingers. Somehow his sarcasm was far more menacing than a tantrum. He clucked his tongue and frowned. "Sounds pretty wild to me, Jules."

Julia's back struck the door.

That was it. If she had any hope of escaping, she had to run. *Now.*

Luke leaned forward on the couch and raised his eyebrows. "Well?"

She spun and threw open the door, then bolted down the hall for the fire stairs.

"Hey!" Luke bellowed. "Get back here!"

Don't look back, Julia commanded herself. *Don't look back.* She dashed into the dark stairwell. Her breath came in heavy gasps. She clattered down the steps, one hand on the cold metal railing—around and around in tight, dizzying circles.

"Julia!" Luke's voice thundered out above her. "What are you *doing?*"

No, no, don't listen. Her head started to spin—from hunger, from exhaustion, from vertigo and fear. But she wouldn't slow down or look up. She simply kept moving. Floor after floor whirled past her. Her footsteps echoed in a jerky rhythm, floating in space as if they belonged to someone else.

"Goddammit! *Julia!*"

Now she could hear other, fainter footsteps as well.

Just two more flights . . .

Dim light appeared: the exit at the bottom of the stairs. So close! The sight of it sent a burst of energy through her wilting body. Holding her breath, she took the last few steps in one leap— then staggered through the door and tripped, falling face first into a pile of dirty snow.

"Whoa!"

Who said that?

"Where do you think *you're* going, honey?" asked an unfamiliar male voice.

Julia rolled over on her back, wiping the icy moisture on her face with her coat sleeve. "I need help," she sputtered. "Can you—"

She froze.

Three pale boys in leather jackets were standing over her.

All were smiling. All had shaved heads. And all bore a frightening resemblance to the kid who had smashed that girl's skull. Any one of them could have *been* that kid.

"You need help, huh?" asked one. "I can help you, sugar. I'm the magic man."

The other two laughed.

"I knew that hanging around this building would pay off," he added. He leaned forward, leering at Julia with a hungry look in his eye. "Like winning the lottery."

Oh, no. Julia shook her head. *Oh, no—*

"Julia, stop, dammit!"

Luke burst through the door, doubled over and panting. His fingers still clutched the bottle of whiskey. "Will you *please* . . ." He stopped.

Julia's eyes flashed from Luke to the boys and back again.

"Back off, Romeo," one of the skinheads ordered.

Luke straightened. His eyes narrowed. "Who the hell are *you?*" he barked.

"What difference does it make?" another one asked, smiling. He reached behind him and pulled a jagged knife from his back pocket. "Beat it."

Julia swallowed, unable to breathe. *God help me. Please.*

"And leave the booze," the third said.

All three of them laughed.

Luke grinned crookedly. He didn't move. His eyes were blank. Julia stared at him. She knew that look on his face; she knew it as well as she knew her own reflection. It was the look he always got the moment before he struck her. It was as if he were transforming from a human being into something else. The smile was his, but the eyes were purely animal: emotionless, predatory. The contrast was terrifying. . . .

Without warning Luke sprang forward and smashed his bottle over the knife-wielding kid's head.

Julia screamed. She stared in petrified shock as the kid collapsed beside her, inches away. Blood began to flow rapidly from a gash in his pasty bald scalp. It mixed in the snow with putrid whiskey and shards of glass. He didn't move. Julia lifted her eyes.

Luke was gazing down at her, breathing hard. He still held the broken bottle neck in his fist. Then he reached down and snatched up the knife, turning to face the other two kids.

"What about you guys?" he whispered. "You want some?"

They didn't answer. They simply turned and sprinted down the deserted street, vanishing around a corner.

Julia followed them with her eyes. Her mind seemed incapable of comprehending what had just happened. It was a blur. It had all passed so quickly. In *seconds*. The fear still clung to her: the fear of being raped, of being beaten, of being *killed*—

"We're getting the hell out of here," Luke snapped.

The next instant Julia found herself being roughly hauled to her feet by her coat lapels. Luke thrust his face inches from her own. His eyes smoldered.

"Do you hear me?" he murmured.

Julia nodded, gulping painfully. She couldn't speak.

"Good." He let her go. She nearly dropped back into the snow.

"Should we—should we go back upstairs?" she stammered.

"Just to get some stuff. But we're leaving the city. Today. Right now."

"We *are?*" she croaked, her eyes widening.

Luke nodded. He began pacing back and forth

agitatedly in the snow, staring down at the motionless skinhead. "If you'd just let me *finish* up there before running off like an *idiot,* none of this would have happened," he snarled. "I was gonna tell you that it's not safe here anymore. But I guess you found that out for yourself. So we're leaving. We're gonna walk across the George Washington Bridge and follow I-95 from there."

She shook her head. "But where . . . where are we going?" she asked in a hollow voice.

He shrugged. "Don't know. Just far away from *here.*" He glanced down the street. "Go upstairs and grab what you can carry. And hurry. Those punks are gonna be back."

She nodded. Her heart was beating so fast, she thought she was going to pass out. This was crazy. So she was going to leave. After all *that.* And it was Luke's idea! This wasn't how she'd imagined it, not in a million years—but at this point she wouldn't fight it. Trying to ditch Luke had been stupid. No, it had been more than that. It had been suicide. The sad and sick truth was that she needed Luke to survive. She couldn't last two seconds without him. *Literally.* It was pathetic. She turned and slunk toward the door.

"Oh, and Jules?"

Luke's hand slithered out like a rattlesnake. Before Julia could even blink, his fingers clamped painfully around her smooth brown wrist.

"One more thing," he murmured. "Don't ever, ever try to run away from me again. 'Cause if you do, I'll kill you. Got it?"

University of Texas Hospital
Austin, Texas
Afternoon of January 7

Harold leaned against the cafeteria door, staring through the small square window at the frightened teenage rabble packed around tables—stuffing themselves, snoring, arguing, crying. . . .

I can't take this anymore, he thought fretfully. *I have to sneak out of here.*

The situation was getting out of hand. By his latest estimate, there were probably four-hundred-odd kids at the hospital now. Of course, his mind might be playing tricks on him. He'd slept maybe fifteen hours total since New Year's Eve. Formless shapes danced at the edges of his vision. He had to put drops in his eyes every hour or so. His bones creaked whenever he moved.

"Where is he?" a panicked girl's voice cried from around the corner. "I have to find him! Where *is* he?"

Not again . . .

A groan passed Harold's lips. He hadn't even had time to *think* in six days. He hadn't left the hospital. He'd been treating kids without pause since the nightmare began. What was the old expression? *Be careful what you wish for because it might come true?* Yes. Well, he'd finally gotten his wish, hadn't he? He'd finally become a full-fledged doctor. He was mending broken bones and pumping stomachs—along with endless other unsavory activities. He had no choice. Every single doctor, nurse, or nurse's assistant had either spontaneously combusted or fled the premises. Conversely, it seemed as if every single survivor had swarmed on the place.

And they were all *teenagers!*

That was the truly bizarre aspect of this whole predicament. Somehow the mysterious disease was selective. As far as he could tell, teenagers, or *some* teenagers, were immune. The result, of course, was that a bunch of traumatized kids now looked to *him* for guidance and comfort. After all, he was older; he was smarter; he was the one with the stethoscope and the white lab coat. So everyone expected him to explain why Mom or Grandpa or little sister Janie vanished in a gruesome pile of black glop.

But what could he say? He didn't know any more than they did. And he needed to figure it out. Soon. He'd already seen three other people—people *his* age—combust in the last few days. The empirical evidence seemed to indicate that time was running out for him, too. . . .

"*There* you are! Oh, thank *God!*"

For what? Harold wondered tiredly. He turned and peered down the hall. A reasonably pretty brunette was hurrying toward him, pushing another girl in a wheelchair—a gorgeous blonde who at first glance appeared to be suffering from cerebral palsy. Her head was lolling to one side. Her limbs were twisted in a grotesque and unnatural position, jerking with an occasional tremor.

The brunette lurched to a stop in front of him. "You're Harold, right?" she panted.

He nodded, studying the blonde's eyes. They were a stunning blue—but at the moment they were dilated, fixed in space, unmoving. No . . . this girl didn't have cerebral palsy. This was a temporary condition. "What happened?" he asked.

"I don't—I don't know," the brunette sputtered. "Larissa was fine, like an hour ago. Me and her were hanging out at her mom's place, looking for food. We found some salami in the fridge. But after we ate it, she started feeling sick. She threw up once. So I looked in the medicine cabinet for some stuff to give her, you know? And I found some pills, and—"

"What kind of pills?" Harold interrupted.

The girl jammed her hand into her jeans pocket, then yanked out a small prescription bottle. She thrust it in Harold's face. Harold squinted at the label.

Compazine.

There's your answer. . . .

"She said her mom always used to take it whenever she felt nauseous or whatever," the girl babbled. "And Larissa isn't allergic to anything. So I figured—"

"Don't worry," Harold stated brusquely.

He grabbed the wheelchair handles and pushed the blonde toward the walk-in medicine closet, resisting the temptation to roll his eyes. So the blonde was having a dystonic reaction to the medication. It was rare—but not surprising, and certainly no cause for panic. Compazine occasionally disagreed with people. A simple shot of Benadryl would eliminate the unpleasant effects. *Morons,* he thought. Why did so many kids assume it was safe to take prescription drugs even if the prescriptions weren't theirs?

"What's going on?" somebody murmured behind him.

"I don't know," the brunette replied anxiously. "My friend is dying. They said this guy Harold was a genius and that he could help her. . . ."

Dying? Harold almost laughed as he pushed the blonde through the door and flicked the light switch. Maybe he should give all these poor saps an elementary medical education. Then maybe they would stop being so melodramatic. Maybe they could start taking care of *themselves* for a change.

The blonde twitched and moaned in her chair.

"Hang on," he mumbled. He tugged open a file cabinet and flipped through some plastic packages of syringes until he found one marked Benadryl. After peeling off the protective wrapping, he held the needle upright in his right hand. With his left he pulled a sterilization packet out of his lab pocket and removed the moist towelette. Then he dabbed it on the girl's trembling forearm.

"Nice and easy," he murmured. Grasping the girl's wrist to hold her still, he jabbed the needle into her moistened flesh and pushed down on the plunger.

The girl blinked. Her muscles instantly relaxed.

Harold sighed.

That's much better now, isn't it?

He removed the needle, rubbed the injection mark with the other side of the towelette, and tossed the used materials into a garbage can. What was her name again? Larissa?

"How do you feel, Larissa?" he asked.

She shook her head, frowned, then gazed up at him. "I feel . . . I don't know." She took a deep breath. "Much better. Wow." A wide smile broke on her face. "*Thank* you."

Harold shrugged. "My pleasure," he murmured. Now that she wasn't twisted up like a pretzel, she looked a hell of a lot better. Yes, yes. As a matter of fact, she was just about the best-looking female who'd wandered in here so far. Young and fresh and ripe. He returned her smile.

"You can stand up if you'd like," he said.

She looked surprised. "Uh . . . okay," she said.

He extended a hand. She took it and gently pushed herself to her feet. Then he led her back out into the hall.

"Larissa?" the brunette cried, as if she didn't believe her eyes.

A crowd of about ten chattering kids had gathered outside the cafeteria door. They fell silent when Harold emerged from the closet.

"My God!" The brunette rushed forward and swept Larissa up in a powerful embrace.

Harold let Larissa's hand go. *Christ.* If only the rest of the cases had been *this* easy. . . .

"It's a miracle!" the brunette exclaimed. She burst into tears. "It's the power of God!"

No, it's the power of Benadryl, Harold thought, but he didn't say anything. Something very curious was happening here, and very suddenly, too. As soon as the brunette started crying the onlookers began to whisper among themselves. Then they stared at Harold. Their expressions slowly changed—from shock, to disbelief . . . and finally to awe.

"How did you do it?" a boy whispered. "How did you do it so fast?"

"You healed her," somebody else drawled in a southern accent. "I saw it. He has the power to heal."

Power to heal? Harold glanced back at Larissa. Even *she* was staring at him now—staring with an eager, almost *reverent* look on her face. He grinned. All of a sudden it didn't seem so far-fetched that she might repay him after all.

"Yes," he proclaimed. "I have the power to heal."

The kids began to nod. *Those poor, lost fools,* Harold thought. They actually *bought* it.

But hey—if they wanted to believe in something, who was *he* to deny them?

CHAPTER
TEN

Babylon, Washington
January 7–13

January 7

So. How do I even start? I'm not used to writing stuff down. I'm used to keeping my thoughts inside my head. That way people can't get to them.

I know that sounds kind of paranoid, but it's true. My own best friend tries to use my thoughts against me all the time. "Ariel," she says, "I know what you're thinking. Don't try to hide it from me." Okay . . . she _used_ to say stuff like that. You know, before the power went out and everybody started melting. Before the world went haywire. Before I lost my father and everything else that's real.

I guess I'm writing this down because I want some kind of proof that all this actually _happened._ It still feels like a dream. Correction: It feels like a really horrible, never-ending, totally heinous nightmare. So if I die or something, which at this point seems pretty likely, I'm hoping that people after me might find this and read it. Then they'll know what happened in the town of Babylon on New Year's Eve, 1998.

You know what's really weird? We still have no way of knowing what happened anywhere else. We're totally cut off. Things might be hunky-dory everywhere else in the world. On the other hand, we might be the only people left alive. Period.

God, that's frightening.

Jez, Brian, Jack, and I have been holed up at my house all week. Trevor has gone out a couple of times, but he hasn't seen much. Just a bunch of scared kids like us. Oh, yeah: He's also seen a bunch of gooey piles of clothes and wrecked cars.

January 8

This morning I stepped outside my house for the first time. I guess I was going a little stir-crazy. Plus we needed some more food and stuff. Brian came with me. We walked around the neighborhood for a couple of hours and stopped at the grocery store. It was empty—cleaned out—except for a bunch of flies and some spoiled meat that stunk up the whole street.

The freakiest thing about it, though, was

how totally _peaceful_ everything looked.
(Well, except for the grocery store and the
clothes and the car wrecks.) For some reason I
expected something different . . . I don't
know, like huge burning pits everywhere and
destroyed buildings and stuff. But everything looked exactly the same as it did
before. It was cold and gray, but it's always
cold and gray in Babylon.

January 9

Man, oh, man . . .
I don't know if I should go for any
more walks. Brian and I left alone, but we
came back with thirteen other kids. Eighteen
people are crashing at our house now!
Trevor was totally pissed, of course. But
it wasn't _my_ fault. It was Brian's. I can't
help it if he's a softie. We went up the road
to watch the sunset over the Pacific Ocean
to get away from the house (i.e., to get away
from Trevor, who was coming on to Jezebel
and making me ill), and we ran into all
these kids from school—Jim O'Hara, his girlfriend, Chad, that whole crew. All _their_
parents were dead, too.
Anyway, they'd just been kind of wandering around town, going from house to house,
looking for food and liquor and stuff.

Brian said that we should all get together in the same place and share the load so all of us won't have to look for stuff all the time. I agreed with him.

And once I suggested my house, I knew that people would come.

I still have clout.

It's kind of funny. See, I don't mean to brag or anything, but I've always been popular or whatever. People look up to me. What can I say? I've got an I-don't-give-a-crap attitude that people respect. (Jesus, I hope the people who read this when I'm dead don't think I'm a totally pretentious, swollen-headed bitch.) I mean, I have to admit, a lot of that attitude is an act. But being a good actress doesn't necessarily mean being a bad person, right? I only show my true sides to the people I trust.

Make that the person I trust.

January 10

Miracle of miracles! Today I actually had fun. Well, for a little while anyway. But I almost managed to forget the state of my life. And right now forgetting about that is the most important thing in the world. I mean it. Shutting out reality is all that matters. For everyone.

89

It all started when Trevor got this stupid idea to check out this experimental mill up at his college. It hasn't been used since the seventies, but he actually thinks he can get it running. (Maybe he's started taking drugs or something.) Anyhow, we got into this huge fight, and he asked me if I had any better ideas. Hell, yeah, I did! I told him that we should all take a trip to the Old Pine Mall, right outside of town. Before I knew it, everybody else was like: "Awesome! We can get free food and free clothes and free anything we want!"

Brian was a little sketched about the whole prospect. He actually still thought we'd be <u>stealing</u> if we took stuff from the mall. I couldn't believe it! My boyfriend is like a saint or something. How can we steal if there's nobody left to steal <u>from</u>? But he changed his mind once we got there.

First of all, the place was completely overrun with kids our age. A lot of them I recognized and a lot of them I didn't. The atmosphere was really weird. It was like a big, desperate, sad, crazy party . . . all at once. About half of the people were laughing and half were crying. They had these huge garbage cans full of really nasty-tasting punch set up in the food court, right under the skylight.

Anyway, once Brian had some of that punch, he forgot all about "stealing."

I guess he and I got pretty wasted. We ended up wandering into this mattress store. Maybe it was a bed store. I don't know. All I know is that it was really dark, and there were plenty of places to crash. There were about a dozen other couples in there already.

We spread out on this deluxe king-sized water bed and just sat there, holding hands and staring into space and listening to other people making out. I know that sounds gross, but it wasn't. Brian started babbling. It was so adorable. He told me that staying with me was the only thing keeping him alive. He told me that he loved me. It was the first time he's ever said that. He said that if we learned anything from this horrible thing, it's that we should love each other. Forever. Not just us either. Everybody. My head was swimming with punch. Listening to his voice was like listening to music.

January 11

Hallelujah! Trevor took off today. Finally. He must have gotten fed up with all the people showing up at our house. I guess some kids at the mall heard that 187 Puget Drive is the hip place to be. News still travels fast around this town. It's kind of nice. In a way it's like . . . I don't know. Things still haven't gotten that out of control. There are still some reminders of the way things used to be. I mean, the rumor network still works, right?

The house is way too crowded, so I moved everybody outside. Brian and Jack built this huge bonfire in the middle of the street. Trevor just watched. He told us that we were "pitiful." He swore he would get the electricity going. He also said a lot of other nasty things, like that I didn't even care that Dad was dead. Where does he get off saying that crap? He hasn't exactly been crying his eyes out either. Screw him! I hope he never comes back.

January 12

I'm starting to get a little worried about Jezebel. She's been sneezing and coughing, and she looks even more pale than usual. I felt her forehead, and it's really warm. Brian the sweetie pie went to the mall to get her some medicine, but the pharmacy was totally cleaned out. He said it looked like a bomb had hit in there. I bet it was those kids in the food court. They probably spiked that punch with whatever drugs they could find. . . .

Trevor made a quick appearance and told us that he was "this close" to getting power going up at the college. I told him to get lost. Why is he wasting our time? We've got bigger worries, like the fact that there are at least a hundred people camped in my front yard, and we're running out of food, and all the grocery stores within ten miles are overrun with bugs.

There's another thing, too. Four kids have melted in the past four days. Brandi Loomis's older sister and three others I didn't know. Nobody has talked about it. I think we were all hoping that we were immune to it. The virus or radiation or whatever. But maybe it's just taking longer to happen to us.

I wonder what it feels like to die like that.

At least we have booze. Jack and three of his buddies broke into this empty bar last night and brought back a huge haul.

That's something, isn't it?

ELEVEN

Puget Drive
Babylon, Washington
Night of January 14

Trevor's sneakers padded softly on the sparkling, moonlit pavement. He felt as if he were floating. Rarely had he been so proud, so satisfied, so *elated*. He'd been walking for a half hour now, but his pace hadn't slowed in the least. The cold night air invigorated him. Even the random piles of clothes and the rusting car wrecks scattered along the winding coastal road had lost their capacity to terrify. He was used to all that now.

It was odd: He'd traveled this same route almost every single day of his entire life, but never had it seemed so beautiful as at this moment— perched on a cliff, lined with stately pine trees on one side and a breathtaking view of Puget Sound on the other. The moon was so bright. He could hear the water crashing against the rocks far below. Its rhythm was like a sound track to his life: a life that had just been validated, made *essential*.

He'd *done* it. He'd actually done it!

He'd restored power to Babylon.

Well, a small part of Babylon anyway. But still: Three dead buildings at the Washington Institute

94

of Technology had been revived. Dozens and dozens of rooms now hummed with electricity and running water—lighted, heated, connected, *alive*. The blackout was over.

Thanks to *him*.

And the solution had been so obvious, hadn't it? He laughed out loud. He had actually been a little surprised that none of his fellow engineering students remembered the old abandoned hydroelectric mill. It wasn't far from campus—only a five-minute walk through the woods, right next to Edmonds Creek. The faculty always made such a big deal out of it, too. "Get it working! We'll have environmentally sound power! We can rewire the whole university, the whole town of Babylon! The creek will provide enough energy for all of us!"

So Trevor wandered up to the campus to check it out. He found about twenty other frightened kids still on the premises. He promptly made them his team. Working around the clock for three straight days, they wired the mill generator to a dining hall, a dormitory, and the communications lab. A little self-contained village! Civilization! They'd even found a bunch of hunting rifles in a toolshed. They could restock their food supply with deer and birds if worst came to worst. It was amazing. They'd already taken the first step toward picking up the pieces of their shattered existence.

But that was his reward for having the ability to focus in the midst of chaos and panic.

Ariel owes me now, he thought gleefully. *All her stupid, drunken friends owe me. They owe me big time. . . .*

He broke into a jog. He could see the thick column of black smoke rising from a spot on the other side of a sharp rise in the road. He was almost home. Adrenaline surged through his veins. Ariel's newfound clique would have no more need for that fire now. Now they needed *him*. Trevor was giving them the gift of survival.

He smiled.

So maybe, just maybe, Jezebel would be a little nicer now.

Maybe she'd pay more attention to him. Maybe she'd finally realize that he *wasn't* a dork—that in fact he was the only one who could save her life.

He paused at the top of the hill, taking a moment to survey the immense blaze of stinking garbage and the ragged mob of teenagers huddled around it right in front of his house. His nose wrinkled. It was all so . . . *primitive*. The kids were like moths, unable to do anything but sit and stare at the roaring flames. And they kept coming, too. There must have been over a hundred of them, twice as many as had been there the night before. Of course, a few of them had been struck with the plague in the last few days, seemingly at random. . . .

Again Trevor wondered: *What happened to all the adults? And all the little children? Did they die—or just run away?*

It was baffling. Whatever had killed all the people definitely *hadn't* been a nuclear bomb. A nuclear bomb detonated in near space might have caused the blackout, but the *deaths* were a result of something else. A biological weapon, probably.

But who was responsible? And why did most of the survivors around here seem to be in their late teens? Were teens somehow immune?

Trevor took a step forward—then stopped.

A girl's voice was coming from the trees on the left side of the road.

He peered into the dark tangle of branches but saw nothing. ". . . promise I'll take care of you. I swear. No matter what happens . . ."

Ariel.

He frowned. Her feathery voice was lost in the crackle of the fire. What was she talking about? And with whom? He needed to get closer. He quickly turned and tiptoed back over the crest of the hill, then crept toward the woods with his back bent in order to keep himself hidden. Obviously she hadn't noticed him yet. She would have said something if she had. He snaked his way through some tree limbs, then silently fell to his hands and knees in the cushion of pine needles that lined the dark forest floor.

". . . know we've gotten into fights and stuff," she was saying. "And we've pissed each other off. But we've got to put that behind us. I'm gonna look after you."

There she is. . . .

He could see her now, about fifteen feet away. She was standing in a moonlit clearing, chugging from a gallon jug of wine, facing somebody who was obscured by a nearby tree trunk. Was it Brian? Judging from Ariel's overly emotional tone, it must be.

"Thanks, Ariel. I mean it."

Jezebel!

Well, well. *This* was proving interesting. He wriggled a few inches closer.

"I mean, you're my best friend," Ariel said. She passed the wine to Jezebel. "I love you, Jez. I mean that. I'm just sorry. I'm sorry it took all this horrible stuff for me to finally say it."

Gimme a break, Trevor thought. He didn't know whether to laugh or to gag. He'd never heard such a load of BS before in his life.

Jezebel gulped down the wine for a few seconds. Then she lurched forward and placed an unsteady hand on one of Ariel's shoulders. Trevor caught a glimpse of her long, dyed black hair, swaying in front of her face.

"I love you, too, sweetie," Jezebel slurred. She sniffed loudly, then sneezed.

Sweetie? Trevor sneered contemptuously.

"Really, Ariel," Jezebel went on. She sounded as if she were about to cry. "I'm the one who should be sorry. I'm so glad we're having this talk. So glad. It's like a load off my mind. We gotta clear the air and start over. We're family now. You, me, Brian, and Jack. Family."

Trevor shook his head. Ah . . . the magic of wine-induced blather. Even if Jezebel *was* hot, she was a total phony. Just like Ariel. He was almost tempted to jump out and remind them of how they'd acted toward each other on New Year's Eve—and on practically every single other night for the past three years. *Family* wasn't a word that leaped to mind.

"You know what's so weird?" Jezebel asked. "We should be in *school* this week."

Ariel nodded, wrapping her arms around herself. "I know. Wanna go back to the fire?"

"Yeah. Hey, how long do you think it's gonna be before Trevor gets the power running? Isn't he supposed to come back tonight and tell us? I mean, I haven't been feeling so hot, you know? I wanna be somewhere warm."

Trevor's ears perked up.

"Don't hold your breath," Ariel muttered. "Trevor likes to pretend that he's a lot smarter than he really is. I mean, have you ever *seen* that mill? It was, like, built by a bunch of hippies in the sixties or something. He's never gonna get it working. The fire will keep you warm."

Jezebel coughed. "I guess you're right."

"Look at it this way." Ariel reached for the bottle and took another swig. "I mean, it wouldn't really be so bad if we never have power again—as long as Trevor stays up at WIT."

Jezebel glanced at her. The two of them started cracking up.

Those bitches!

Trevor clenched his fists, crushing two handfuls of dried pine needles into dust. He'd never been so outraged—*ever*. But they would pay for their stupidity. All of them would pay. He would show them who was smart and who wasn't. He was boss now. He had control. And if they didn't want to see him again, fine. They wouldn't have to. He'd ban them from the campus. Even better. He'd tell his friends back up at WIT to *shoot* any trespassers. After all, he had a few guns now, didn't he?

"Ariel!" he barked, pushing himself to his feet.

The two girls whirled around. Trevor stormed toward them, violently swatting stray branches out of his path. Even in the darkness he could tell they were scared—wide-eyed and slack jawed. Good. They *should* be scared.

"Trevor?" Ariel asked, quickly glancing at Jezebel in disbelief. "What are you doing here?"

"I came here to tell you something," he snarled. "I got the power going at WIT."

"You *did?*" she gasped.

"That's right. And there's something else, too. I want you to stay the hell away."

Ariel swallowed. "Why?" She shot Jezebel another confused glance. "What are you—"

"Because I've been working my ass off!" he snapped. "And you've been sitting here on your butt for two weeks, getting plowed. So I'm not letting you in. Either of you. You don't deserve it." He thrust a finger at Ariel's face. "I'm ordering my friends to shoot you if you even come *close* to the buildings. Your boyfriends, too."

"That's crazy," Ariel breathed, stepping away from him.

Jezebel started shaking her head. "Trevor, come on," she pleaded. "You can't do that."

"I can't?" He laughed. "Hey, Jez—get with the program. *I'm* the one who got the electricity going. *I'm* the one with the guns." He leaned in close to her, his voice falling to a whisper. "I can do whatever I goddamn please."

TWELVE

13 Hamesh Orerim
Jerusalem, Israel
Afternoon of January 16

"All praises to Allah!" a hysterical young voice
shouted from the TV in the next room. "The infi-
dels will perish in flame! Lay down your arms!
Allah u akhbar . . ."

Sarah hunched over her spiral notebook at the
tiny breakfast table in Elijah's cramped kitchen,
desperately trying to ignore the racket. Her pen
hovered over the lined paper, poised to write. But
she couldn't concentrate. That voice was like the
incessant barking of a mad dog.

Why did Josh insist on blaring the TV at all hours?
It wasn't as if they were learning anything new. So a
bunch of teenage Islamic fundamentalists were occu-
pying one of the local television stations. Big deal.
Tomorrow Sarah could just as likely find herself listening to the insane rantings of some ultra-Orthodox
Jewish kids or a Christian militia—even a bunch of
Satanists. This particular station had changed hands
five times already in the last ten days.

Oh, just deal with the noise, she scolded herself. *You agreed to let Josh watch.*

Taking a deep breath, she forced herself to continue:

In the absence of any authority, the streets of the Jewish Quarter are growing increasingly dangerous. Fierce fighting among rival religious and ethnic factions has already claimed the lives of dozens of people.

But with no victor in sight, anarchy and lawlessness prevail. The government has ceased to exist. Phone lines are down; contact with the rest of the world is still impossible. Food is scarce. Shops have been stripped of their goods. Only clothing remains plentiful — the remnants of the victims of the mysterious plague. No home or building is safe, not even places of worship. The synagogue at the end of Hamesh Orerim lies in burning ruins. Roving gangs of

Sarah paused for a moment. She wanted to say "roving gangs of teenagers"—but some of the gang members might be older. She wasn't sure.

And she only wanted to record the *facts*. This wasn't a diary. She wasn't going to speculate about things she didn't know. She *knew* the synagogue at the end of Hamesh Orerim had been destroyed because Elijah *lived* at the end of Hamesh Orerim. If she raised her head and glanced out the kitchen window, she could still see flames licking at the white rubble, now tinted gold in the fading afternoon sun.

Roving gangs of young people are plundering their way through the city: stealing, killing, and looting. Perhaps they are partially responsible for the decimation of the children and adult populations. Few seem to remain in the city except juveniles. Most of them have been transformed into fanatics, battling to the death over their version of the Apocalypse: whether it's God's Judgment, the End of Days, the Second Coming, the Wrath of Allah

The pen clattered to the table. She was speculating again. This *wasn't* a diary! How many times did she have to remind herself of that? If this were a diary, she might as well write about eating dry cereal for two straight weeks. She might as well write about journeying through battle-torn Jerusalem only to find every hospital abandoned or about how she couldn't stand to look in the mirror anymore because her face was lashed with scars from the crash. If this were a diary, it would be filled with all her irrational theories about the plague. It would be filled with her growing fears about Josh—who hadn't said a word about trying to get back to New York, who was still ransacking the house for Elijah's nonexistent "black box."

But it wasn't a diary.

It was a journal. A professional, detached, unemotional journal. And writing in this journal was the only thing keeping her sane—

The television abruptly fell silent.

"Sarah!" Josh called from the living room. He sounded breathless, excited. "I think I might have found something! Come here!"

Sarah shook her head. *How many times have I heard that in the last week?* she wondered. It was getting ridiculous. Elijah's house was pretty tiny—only three rooms on one floor: the kitchen, the living room, and a bedroom with a small adjoining bathroom. But Josh refused to give up his search. Where else could he possibly look?

"Come *here!*" he demanded.

Sighing, Sarah pushed herself away from the table and stood. Didn't he know he was just setting himself up for another big disappointment? She had taken a step toward the kitchen door when something outside the window caught her eye.

Uh-oh.

Four girls were standing next to the smoldering remains of the synagogue, talking and gesturing toward Elijah's house. They all wore strange, loose-fitting gowns spun from thick black cloth. And they all had very large machine guns strapped over their shoulders.

"Sarah!" Josh yelled.

The girls began to remove clips of ammunition from the folds of their robes.

Sarah burst into the garbage-strewn living room. She didn't know *who* those girls were or to which gang or faction they belonged—but it didn't matter. Their intentions were clear. They were coming into this house.

"*There* you are," Josh said. He was on his hands and knees, rummaging through the closet by the front door. "Come here—"

"Quiet!" Sarah hissed, crouching by his side. Her eyes darted to the living room window. Outside, the girls were loading the ammunition clips into their guns. Sarah clasped a hand over her chest, suddenly aware that her heart was pounding.

"Check this out," Josh continued, oblivious to the fact that anything was wrong. He knocked once on the floorboard of the closet. The noise was deep and resonant, indicating a hollow space underneath. "I can't believe I missed this earlier—"

"Josh, *please* shut up," Sarah murmured imploringly. She kept her gaze pinned to the girls.

They were marching toward the front walk now, their machine guns gripped tightly with both hands, their fingers on the triggers. . . .

Josh stuck his head deep into the closet. "I think this little thingy might be a lever."

Sarah shot him a hard glare. But he kept rustling. There was a fumbling noise and a soft *click,* and then he withdrew his head from the closet.

Sarah's eyes widened.

The floorboards had fallen open, revealing a rusted metal ladder that led to a rough-hewn stone floor maybe ten feet below. She couldn't believe it. But this wasn't the time to ponder the reasons why Elijah had never mentioned a trapdoor or a cellar.

"Get in!" she breathed.

Josh turned to face her, frowning. "Why—"

"Just *do* it!" she hissed, shoving him forward. "And don't say another word."

Trembling, Josh eased himself through the opening and scrambled down into the hole. Sarah swallowed. She could hear footsteps scraping on the front walk. The girls were right outside. She pulled the closet door shut behind her. Her insides tightened. She slid through the opening and lowered her feet onto the ladder, then grasped the top rung and started climbing down, hand over hand, as fast as she could. Three feet from the bottom, she reached up and swung the trapdoor shut over her head.

The front door crashed open.

Sarah held her breath.

Heavy boots pounded on the floor above her.

She clung to the ladder, not moving a muscle, staring unblinkingly at the bottom of the trapdoor.

The footsteps spread throughout the house—into the bedroom and the kitchen.

"Nobody's here," a girl said. Her voice was muffled and far away, but her tone was sharp. She had a cultured British accent. "Looks like somebody looted the place already."

Thank God Josh made such a mess, Sarah found herself thinking. She allowed herself a quick peek at him. He was staring at the trapdoor too, his mouth agape. Sarah glanced around the cellar. The ladder stood at the mouth of a long stone passageway, sloping downward under the house toward a hidden source of light. "Do you think someone found it?" another girl asked. She, too, had a British accent.

"It doesn't matter," the first answered. "Elijah Levy was the only one alive who could decipher the code."

Sarah nearly gasped. *They know Elijah!*

"What about his grandniece?" the second girl asked. "Do you think she was here?"

"Doubtful," the first replied. "She lives in Tel Aviv. But she's of no importance."

Horrified, Sarah locked gazes with Josh. For a moment she thought she might faint. *Who are these people? How do they know who I am?*

"What should we do?" a third voice asked.

"Torch the place," the first stated. "If the scroll is here, it will provide a fitting burnt offering for Lilith."

The footsteps clattered out of the house.

Sarah's mind whirled. *Torch the place?*

There was a tinkle of shattering glass, followed by the sound of something rolling across the floor.

Uh-oh. She could guess what that meant. . . .

"Run, Josh!" she whispered, dropping to the passage floor.

Without a moment's hesitation he sprinted down the slope toward the light. Sarah dashed after him, close on his heels. They rounded a corner—

Kaboom!

An explosion shook the earth. Sarah was hurtled to the ground. She threw her arms over her head. A shower of dust and small rocks rained down on her. She cringed, expecting to be smothered. But after what seemed like an eternity, the air fell silent.

When she finally lifted her eyes, she found herself in a large, empty stone chamber.

No . . . not quite empty. She blinked. There was something there, not five feet away from her.

It was a small ebony chest, illuminated by a single shaft of light from a hole in the ceiling.

PART III:

"Flesh she will eat, and blood she will drink!" the sweet young voices chanted again and again, in a language long forgotten by all those except the initiated. "Flesh she will eat, and blood she will drink. . . ."

Naamah stood at the center of the stone circle, basking in the light of the moon and the singsong lilt of her hooded flock. Her Lilum.

The Demon would be coming soon.

After three thousand years Lilith had finally awakened.

The sun had reached out and revived her spirit.

The sun had started the clock on her secret and ancient weapon. Nothing could stop its ticking now.

The countdown had begun.

The sun had opened the latent inner eyes of the Visionaries as well, but Naamah was not concerned. The Demon had a plan for them, a plan subtle and seductive. A false prophet, a "healer," would rise to lead them astray. A man, no less. The Third Prophecy foretold it.

The Prophecies were Truth.

In all her eighteen years Naamah never dreamed that the First Prophecy would be fulfilled with such swiftness and such wrath. The flare had brought confusion, wiping out power in some cities while leaving others miraculously unscathed. And the flare had given the Lilum power over life and death. The Death had come and would continue to come, striking down all the aged and the young with equal and indiscriminate fury.

The Death was man-made, yes. But only the Demon's genius and power of foresight could have unleashed it.

Naamah's concern now was the Chosen One.

The Chosen One was no Visionary. She did not even know she had been born to lead the enemies of Lilith. She would not believe she was the Soashyant— the Savior incarnate. She knew herself to be too selfish, too judgmental.

But the Prophecies foretold that she would learn, she would grow, and she would be transformed.

She would come forth and meet Lilith upon the final battlefield.

For now, however, the Chosen One was struggling with her own trivial crises, unaware of her ultimate role in the end of human history. . . .

THIRTEEN

Pittsburgh City Jail
Pittsburgh, Pennsylvania
January 4–17

The day after Eight Ball split, George managed to pull himself through the hole in the gate and drag himself down the hall to a lounge area. It took nearly four hours. His right ankle had swollen up like a big blue balloon. There was soft wall-to-wall carpeting and some coats he could use as blankets—and a big refrigerator loaded with ham sandwiches and soda and leftover pizza. There was also a jacket filled with packets of cocaine and pills. That night George had a rousing dinner of codeine, Sprite, and four soggy slices of cold pepperoni pie. Then he slept soundly for the first time in days.

"Hello?" he called the next morning. His voice echoed off the cold cinder block walls.

"Hello? Anybody here?" But there was no answer. Maybe all the prisoners had escaped, like Eight Ball. Or maybe they'd all melted away, like the cop. It didn't really matter one way or the other. He had the place to himself.

The phone rang one afternoon. It rang for almost five minutes. George thought that was funny. Why would anybody call an empty jail? He wanted to pick it up. But the phone was on the wall—just beyond his reach from the floor. Too bad. He had his answer all planned out.

"This is George Porter," he would have said. "*I'm* in charge now."

Hours melted into hours, days melted into days, and time became a blur of pain, hunger, and dreams. The line between sleep and consciousness faded. Eventually it disappeared altogether. George simply allowed himself to drift. He floated in empty space, or back through the corridors of his childhood, or into some bizarre place where the air was thick with a foul stench and somebody kept forcing rubbery slices of stale meat down his throat.

He wasn't alone anymore. Or was he? He was dimly aware of another presence, a form or shape just outside the field of his cloudy vision. Maybe it was just a nightmare. He was still having nightmares. Occasionally, very occasionally, he would see himself standing on top of that black cliff, watching his unborn baby plunge into the sea. . . .

If my baby dies, the Demon will triumph. I have to go west. I have to find the Chosen One. Only the Chosen One can save my baby.

"Hey, George?"
George awoke with a start.
"You're up. Whew."

George's body immediately stiffened. He was lying in a strange bed, face-to-face with some weird guy he'd never seen before.

"How are you feeling?" the guy asked quietly.

A scowl instinctively crossed George's face. Who *was* this dude? And why was he sitting so close? He was older—maybe in his early twenties—kind of burly, with a thick brown beard and a ponytail. He had on a wool Steelers cap. He looked like a mountain man or something, wearing a flannel shirt and overalls. And his eyes . . . there was something about them George didn't trust. They were big and brown and way too friendly.

"How do you know my name?" George demanded. His voice sounded foreign to his own ears: deep and scratchy.

"You told me your name." The guy smiled. "I told you mine, too. It's Doug." He paused, studying George's expression. "But I guess you don't remember. You've been pretty out of it."

George glared at the guy, weighing his words. *Doug?* No, he sure as hell didn't know any Doug. His eyes roved across the cramped, brightly lit room—instantly recognizing it as another jail cell, the kind designed for an extended incarceration. But how had he gotten here? He was lying under the covers in a narrow bed. There was a sink and toilet on the other wall, not six feet away. *Doug,* or whoever he was, had pulled up a wooden chair. A huge red cooler sat right beside him on the floor. The cell door was open.

"What's the last thing you remember?" Doug asked.

"I *don't* remember you," George spat.

Doug held up his hands. "It's okay," he said softly. "Just relax. I kinda figured you wouldn't. You don't need to be scared, though. I just want to make sure you're okay."

"I'm not scared," George muttered, edging away from him on the mattress.

Doug nodded soberly. "Okay, okay." He stood up and leaned against the sink, putting as much distance between them as possible. "I'm just glad you're snapping out of it. Tell me how your ankle feels."

George frowned. He hadn't even *noticed* his ankle. He sat up and felt for the cracked bone under the covers. Much to his surprise, his fingers brushed against some sort of thick, rough padding. He shot a puzzled look at Doug.

"I bandaged it," Doug explained. "See, when I found you, it was really swollen. There was some first aid stuff in the infirmary. So I iced it down, then—"

"Hold up, man," George interrupted. "What do you mean, when you *found* me?"

"I came in here a few days ago, looking for food." He laughed once. "I figured it would be safe. I mean, who would want to hide out in a jail? Anyway, I was just wandering around, checking it out—and I found you in that room upstairs. You were in really bad shape. So I cleaned you up and bandaged your ankle. Then I brought you down here. I've been watching you and feeding you ever since."

George just kept staring at the guy, processing his

words. *Watching me and feeding me.* So this Doug dude had found him and fixed him up. That much he understood. But why? It sounded too easy. Doug was obviously in some kind of danger if he needed to hide out. And did he want something from George?

"What do you mean, you figured it would be safe?" George asked.

Doug opened his mouth, then hesitated. He stroked his beard. "Lemme ask you something. How long have you been here?"

"Since New Year's Eve," he answered cautiously.

"New Year's Eve, huh?" Doug raised his eyebrows. "Before or after?"

"Before or after *what?*"

"Before or after everybody vaporized," Doug said.

George swallowed. *Jesus.* That's right. He'd almost forgotten about the way that cop had died. He must have been trying to shut the memory out of his mind. But now he remembered. Yeah, he remembered, all right. It made him want to retch.

"Before," he finally answered.

"You see any of it?" Doug asked.

George nodded. He didn't feel so hot all of a sudden. "I guess. I mean, I saw something happen to the cop who locked me down."

"Was he the one who messed up your ankle?"

"Uh . . . no." George shook his head. "I messed it up trying to bust out of here."

Doug grinned. "Looks like you managed."

George shrugged. He figured he'd leave out the part about how Eight Ball had punched through the gate and left him here to rot. Doug didn't need

116

to hear the whole story. But for a second George wondered what happened to old Eight Ball. Did he also . . . *vaporize?*

"So, uh—what happened?" George asked.

Doug's grin vanished. "Nobody knows. A whole lot of people died, though. Almost everybody. All at once, too. You know, you were pretty lucky to be holed up in here this whole time. It's a free-for-all out there. Every man for himself. I guess Pittsburgh is one of the few places that has electricity, so people have been coming here to make the most of it. Kids, mostly." He laughed again—but the sound was harsh and cold, with no humor. "It's funny. Me and my buddies always used to talk about what it would be like if the world came to an end. Now we know." His eyes locked on the younger boy's. "It sucks."

George couldn't answer. Almost *everybody* was dead? What did that *mean?* He was suddenly having trouble breathing. His chest felt constricted. He couldn't listen to this. It must be a lie. It was too crazy. . . .

Doug sighed. "Look, George, I'll leave you alone. I just wanted to make sure you were all right." He pushed himself off the sink and pointed at the cooler. "There's a bunch of sandwiches and drinks and stuff in there—enough to last a few days. I'd stay off your foot until then. I don't think it's broken, but it's a real bad sprain." He headed toward the door. "Take care of yourself—"

"Wait!" George cried, suddenly terrified. He couldn't be *alone,* not after having heard all that. "I mean, where . . . uh, you're leaving?"

117

Doug nodded grimly. "I gotta get out of this place. My girlfriend—" His voice broke. For a moment he look pained. Then he drew in his breath. "My girlfriend lives out west," he finally managed. "I'm gonna try to find her."

Out west! A flash of recognition exploded in George's brain. The visions . . . the visions told him to go west. His life depended on it. *Many* lives depended on it. And even if he were just going insane, there was still no reason to stick around here. His foster family, his friends—they were probably all dead. Who was he kidding? He never really liked any of those jerks anyway.

"Are you sure you're okay?" Doug asked from the doorway.

"I'm coming with you."

The words popped out of George's mouth even before he knew he was saying them. But any lingering suspicion of Doug had vanished. Doug was just a guy who'd helped him, for no other reason than to help a stranger in trouble. George was sure of that now.

"I'd bring you if I could, pal," Doug said ruefully. "Believe me. I could use the company. But I'm going on foot." He glanced at George's ankle. "And you're not exactly—"

"You're not going on foot," George cut in. He smiled. "You're driving."

Doug cocked an eyebrow. "But I don't have a car. Do you?"

"Nope. But I will. As soon as you help me get to the parking lot."

"How's that?" Doug asked dubiously. "I don't—"

"Don't worry," George insisted. "Just think of it as a favor for saving my life."

It took about ten minutes of hopping around on his left foot in the freezing cold before George found a car to his liking. It was a shiny red Corvette. It figured: Cops loved fast American cars. The doors were unlocked, of course. Who would break into a cop's car in the middle of a jailhouse parking lot? George slid into the driver's seat and punched the steering column with the butt of his palm until the casing popped open. Then he quickly and expertly connected the transmission wires. The engine roared to life. The entire procedure lasted no more than ten seconds. He grinned at Doug.

"I was busted for hot-wiring," he said proudly.

The highway stretched out before them in the night, snowy and deserted except for a few wrecks here and there, rushing under the headlights as they climbed high into the mountains. George gazed out the passenger side window. The dark landscape was a blur. They hadn't seen a soul since they'd left the city limits. George hadn't said anything about the absence of people, though; neither of them had spoken. At least it felt good to be in this car, good to be safe and warm and snug, good to be moving. He'd never been outside of Pittsburgh before.

"So where are we going anyway?" he asked, breaking the silence. He wrapped his arms around himself in the leather cop jacket he'd found back at the jail.

Doug didn't answer.

George turned and glanced at him. Doug was gripping the steering wheel tightly.

"Well?" George asked.

"I lied to you," Doug said, without taking his eyes from the road.

Uh-oh. George's stomach lurched. Maybe he'd been wrong about Doug. . . .

"I'm not looking for my girlfriend," Doug continued. His voice quavered. "My girlfriend is . . . she's dead. I was—I was with her when she died." He turned to George for an instant, then back to the road. His face was colorless. "She died New Year's Eve. She came back to celebrate my birthday with me. My birthday's on the seventh. I . . . uh, turned twenty-one. She wanted to make it . . . special."

George swallowed. *Man.* That was *harsh.* He felt a weird rush of relief and horror at the same time. If Doug was making this up, he was a damn good actor. No, this was the truth. He'd been "with" his girlfriend New Year's Eve. But what did he mean, really? *With*—like doing it? Had she turned into a puddle of black ooze while they were . . .

"She wasn't one of the lucky ones," Doug added.

George shivered. "Maybe she *was,*" he found himself muttering. "I'm sorry, man."

Doug sighed deeply. "That's okay. Anyway, the reason I'm going out west is . . . I don't know; I can't explain it. It's because I feel like I *have* to."

George's heart bounced. "What do you mean?" he whispered.

"Promise me you won't tell me I'm crazy?" Doug demanded.

George shook his head. "No way."

"Ever since New Year's Eve . . ." He took a deep breath. "Ever since New Year's Eve, I've had these weird flashes."

"Me too!" George exclaimed. He felt as if a switch had been thrown, as if an electric connection had been made. This was *serious*. This was *major*.

"Yeah?" Doug licked his lips nervously. "What are yours like?"

"I see myself standing on this cliff," George explained, unable to contain his excitement. "And I have this baby. Which is totally impossible. I mean, I never even . . ." *Oh, brother.* He stopped in midsentence, suddenly embarrassed. He turned back to the window. "I mean, I'm only sixteen," he mumbled.

Doug laughed quietly. "Don't worry, George. I didn't get laid till I was in college."

For some reason that comment only made George feel like more of a fool. He didn't want to talk about himself anymore. "Well, anyways, that's about it," he said. "What happens in *your* visions?"

"They don't make any sense," Doug said. "I mean, I see myself with this angel. At least I *think* it's an angel. It's this guy in a white robe. But he's hurt. And a voice calls to me, telling me that I have to save the angel to help the Chosen One. . . ."

The Chosen One! George held his breath. He hadn't *seen* the Chosen One yet, but he knew about her. Somehow he knew. This too was crucial.

Doug kept him waiting.

George exhaled. "Go *on,*" he demanded impatiently. He turned toward the wheel.

But Doug was dying.

There had been no warning, no clue, nothing. He just started melting away.

George watched, unable to move. Doug's skin had already liquefied. His body seemed to crumple in on itself. His overalls and flannel shirt gently tumbled toward the seat, smothering the black, bubbling flesh as they fell. His slimy fingers slid from the steering wheel. Blood spurted out onto the windshield. Still he didn't make a sound—not a cry of pain or surprise.

"Doug?" George breathed, even though he knew it was pointless.

Finally he reached out and grabbed the wheel. Then he kicked his left foot over the gearshift and then slammed it down on the brake. The tires screeched. He was thrown against the dashboard, but the thick jacket softened the blow.

The car seemed to skid for a long time.

By the time it finally came to a halt on the vacant highway, George was alone.

FOURTEEN

WIT Campus
Babylon, Washington
Morning of January 26

"He's not gonna shoot you!" Jack yelled over the freezing rain. "You're his sister! Just go up there and tell him that we're sorry. Tell him that we promise to be good and help out and stuff. No more booze."

Ariel shook her head. There was no way Trevor was going to let them inside. She shoved her raw fingers deep inside her grimy overcoat. Icy raindrops pounded heavily on the fabric and on her sodden wool hat. Her brownish-blonde hair was soaked. It was hopeless. She knew her brother better than any of them. He was *twisted*. Somebody had already taken a few potshots at Brian last week. The bullets hadn't come close, but the message was clear. *Keep out*. Her teeth chattered as she stared across the muddy field at the fuzzy lights of the dormitory, glowing faintly through the storm. It must be so warm and cozy in there. . . .

"Come on, Ariel," Jezebel begged. She'd been using that annoying, whiny-little-girl voice for the past two weeks. She sniffed once. "Please? I'm really, really sick. I've had a fever for *weeks* now. It's serious, okay?"

123

"That's why I *told* you we shouldn't have left my house," Ariel growled.

"Just try talking to Trevor," Jack insisted.

And get shot? Ariel silently retorted. The dismal weather was trying her patience, chilling her bones. It was so stupid to have come here. Not to mention frustrating. She hopped up and down a few times in the slush in a desperate effort to get her blood flowing. But she just ended up splashing herself. She glanced down at her mud-soaked sneakers. They weren't waterproof; they weren't made for this kind of abuse. Her feet were freezing. She had to get home.

Why hadn't they seen this coming? They'd known the food supply would run out a long time ago. But still they kept eating and partying, not caring. . . .

"Look, we'll just make ourselves crazy if we hang out here any more," Brian said after a moment. He stepped through the slush and put a soggy arm around Ariel, pulling her close. "We're all gonna catch pneumonia. We can go to my place. Build another fire—"

"Brian, wait!" Jezebel whispered. She pointed toward the dormitory. "Look!"

Ariel squinted through the downpour. A lone, heavily bundled figure had just left the building. He was marching across the field—straight toward them, with a rifle held at his side. That awkward, top-heavy stride was unmistakable.

"Is that Trevor?" Jack asked.

Ariel shivered. "Yup."

Brian squeezed her shoulder. "What do you think he wants?"

"Maybe he wants to shoot us," Ariel muttered.

Trevor kept coming. He was close enough now so that she could see his face: those familiar red cheeks and hook nose. His narrow lips were set in a disdainful scowl. He stopped about fifteen paces from where they were standing, then lifted and cocked the rifle. Even in the pouring rain Ariel could hear the sharp snap of metal.

"Jezebel?" Trevor called.

Jezebel glanced at Ariel, clearly bewildered.

"Yeah?" she answered meekly without looking at him.

"You can come with me if you want," he stated.

Her eyes narrowed. "What do you mean?" she asked. She sounded apprehensive.

"Exactly what I said." His tone was flat. He waved the rifle at them. "You can come with me. Just you."

"That *bastard*," Jack hissed.

Ariel glanced from Jezebel to Trevor and back again. Jezebel was biting her lip. She cast furtive, longing looks at the dormitory. And Trevor was staring at her with a lustful glint in his eye. Ariel shook her head. How could her brother have sunk so low? It was sickening. But she knew right then that Jezebel wouldn't refuse Trevor's offer. She was too weak, too scared for her own life.

So much for our little "family," Ariel thought bitterly.

"Make up your mind," Trevor demanded. "I'm getting cold."

Jezebel took a step forward.

"Jez!" Jack snapped. "What are you *doing?*"

Ariel sighed. "Let her go," she murmured, leaning

125

against Brian. She supposed she should have known that the tenuous pact between Jezebel and her would never last. Trevor had known.

At least I have Brian, was all she could think. *And that's more important than anyone else could know.*

Jezebel looked at the ground, then back at Jack. Her face was very pale. Her black hair hung in wet, stringy clumps in front of her eyes.

"Look, I'm just gonna go in there until I get better, okay?" she whispered. "As soon as my cold is gone, I'm gonna leave. And I'm gonna try—"

"Screw you," Jack muttered. He whirled around and stared in the opposite direction, folding his arms across his chest. "Fine. Go. Just get the hell out of my sight."

Jezebel swallowed. She reached for his shoulder but stopped. Her hand fell to her side. She looked to Ariel—as if for validation or at least for a flicker of forgiveness. *What other choice do I have?* her pleading expression seemed to ask.

But Ariel didn't answer. She couldn't. Her features remained blank.

The silence stretched between them.

Rain lashed the ground, their clothes, their faces.

"Jezebel!" Trevor shouted.

Jezebel hesitated—then bolted across the field. Huge drops of muddy water splashed around her ankles. She didn't stop either. She ran right past Trevor . . . straight for the dormitory door. An instant later she vanished into the warm light.

Trevor followed her with his eyes. Then he turned and smiled at Ariel.

"You know, you're lucky I didn't shoot you," he called. He sounded relaxed and easygoing—as if he were talking about a board game instead of real life. "I've been watching you all morning through binoculars. I could have killed every one of you. Next time I will."

He turned and jogged back in Jezebel's footsteps.

Ariel lowered her gaze.

The dormitory door slammed, a distant echo.

I wonder what Dad would say if he were alive, Ariel found herself thinking. *I wonder what he would think of his son.*

"You know what's so screwed up?" Jack suddenly asked. His voice was strained.

Ariel glanced up at him. She couldn't believe it. He was *crying.*

A wave of sorrow and regret washed over her. It was absurd: She'd never wanted to console someone as much as she wanted to console Jack at this moment. Big, dumb, thick Jack. But she couldn't console him—for reasons past as well as present. And she hated herself for it. Too much mistrust lay between them, too much enmity. Even now.

Brian stepped away from Ariel and placed a hand on Jack's back. "What's screwed up, man?" he asked gently.

"Tomorrow's my *birthday,*" Jack choked out. He glanced at Ariel and Brian, then rubbed his face and sniffed. "My twenty-first birthday." He laughed through his tears. "You know, I never thought it was gonna be like this."

Oh, Jack . . .

Ariel rushed forward and threw her arms around him.

Screw the past, she thought, giving in to her abandon. *I'm starting over.*

"We'll go home, okay?" she murmured. She squeezed him tightly. He squeezed her back. She swallowed hard. But she wasn't going allow herself to cry—for Jack's sake. "Let's go to Brian's and build that fire, and I'll rustle up some cake mix, and we'll make a cake, okay?"

"Okay," Jack croaked. He trembled slightly. "Think we can rustle up some tequila, too?"

Ariel withdrew from his sopping wet embrace and grinned at him. "I guarantee it."

"Good." A sad smile crossed his lips. "I could use a drink right now. . . ." His smile disappeared.

"You gonna be okay?" Brian asked.

Jack shook his head.

He stared at the ground, as if he'd lost something.

All at once his hands flew to his throat. His face contorted in agony.

Ariel stepped back. "Jack?"

He fell to his knees, staring up at her in horror. The all too familiar black bubbles had appeared on his face.

No. Not Jack. Not now . . .

But even as these thoughts festered in her brain, the plague worked its swift and inexorable dissolution, transforming Jack into a runny pile of rain-soaked clothes before her eyes. Ariel whirled and buried her face in Brian's shoulder. She wished

128

she were blind, deaf, *anything*. Then she wouldn't be able to see or hear or experience the world around her. . . .

"That's it," Brian hissed, holding her close.

"What is?" she breathed.

"We gotta get away from here."

Ariel stepped apart from her boyfriend and stared at him. The softness in his voice was gone— replaced with a harsh and totally unfamiliar edge.

"We're gonna go south, where it's warm," Brian stated. He gazed blankly into space. "Screw Trevor. I can't afford to live the way I've lived anymore. We're gonna wait till spring. Then I'm gonna come back here and burn this place to the ground. I swear to God I will."

FIFTEEN

East Jerusalem, Israel
Afternoon of January 30

In the days following the destruction of Elijah's house, Sarah refused to look at the crumbling parchment scroll hidden in that black box. She simply convinced herself that she had more important things to do. Namely she had to ensure her own survival and the survival of her brother. Simply convincing Josh to *leave* the underground chamber had been a major feat. But finally hunger had driven the two of them outside—through the burning streets of the Jewish Quarter, out of the gates of the Old City, and into the hills of East Jerusalem . . . where they'd stumbled on an abandoned army barracks.

They'd been there ever since. Josh insisted that they stay close to the city. And the barracks *seemed* safe.

Sarah, however, didn't feel safe at all.

She'd hardly slept, in fact. Finding such a well-stocked new home was just a little too lucky, a little too *convenient*, wasn't it? Why wasn't anybody else here? True, the weapons were gone—but there was plenty of food. The kitchen was in good working order. There was even a VCR in one of the common areas. Fifty people could live here for a month, easily. In comfort, no less. So why was it empty? Was it a trap, deliberately set for them? Maybe it was. No possibility seemed too far-fetched.

Every day Sarah roamed the empty halls with a butcher knife, fully expecting to confront a gun-wielding girl in a black robe.

And every day Joshua sat in the dead commandant's office, poring over Elijah's ancient manuscript as if it might somehow magically deliver them from this nightmare and whisk them home, back to the warm embraces of their parents.

And what did Sarah know? Maybe it *would*.

That was the real reason she wouldn't look at the scroll. She was *afraid* of it. She was afraid of the mysterious prophecies Josh had told her it contained. The tiny scrawl of Hebrew letters perfectly symbolized the jumble of uncertainty, of *guesswork*, that her world had become. There was nothing left in her life about which she could state unequivocally: "This is *truth*." Nothing. No facts remained, other than that millions of people were dead, Jerusalem was falling apart—and a very dangerous group of strangers knew about her, her family, and this scroll.

"Sarah?"

Josh's faint voice echoed down the stone corridor from behind the closed office door.

"Sarah, can you come take a look at this?"

She paused in midstep, clutching the butcher knife tightly. She stared down at the serrated blade. The metal caught a flash of the afternoon sun streaming through the dusty windows.

"Sarah?"

"What is it, Josh?" she called reluctantly.

"I want you to take a look at this section. I don't think I'm reading it right. And you speak Hebrew better than I do."

"That's not true," she replied—even though it was.

"Just come here, Sarah, all right?" he demanded.

She turned to face the door, but her feet would budge no further. "I'm . . . I'm busy."

"Doing *what?*" He sounded exasperated. "Why won't you just *look* at the scroll?"

"Because I don't want to," she snapped.

There was a pause. Then she heard the screech of a chair sliding across the floor. The office door burst open. Josh stormed down the hallway, clutching the wooden pegs of the scroll in either hand.

Oh, Jesus . . .

"Just *look* at this," he ordered. "It's not gonna kill you."

How do you know? she thought, but she didn't say anything.

Josh stepped up beside her and unrolled a small segment of the scroll in front of her face. She cast a quick glace at him, struck for a moment by how *skinny* he looked. His jawline had grown sharp, gaunt. His cheekbones stood out in stark relief against the pallid flesh of his face. He wasn't eating enough. He needed to take better care of himself.

"What?" he demanded.

"Nothing," she murmured. She wrenched her eyes away from him and onto the frayed paper. "So what can't you read?"

"That part at the bottom. See it?"

Sarah leaned forward and peered closely at the hundreds of tiny characters inscribed in black ink. The text was divided in large blocks, much like the Torah. But in the portion Josh had unrolled there was a break underneath one of the blocks, separating a small paragraph from the rest of the main passage.

"That little part under the break?" she asked.

Josh nodded. "Yeah."

Sarah took a deep breath and squinted at the words, reading right to left and translating out loud as she read. "'Being . . . heavenly . . . lifts' . . . or I guess that could be 'raises us.'" She paused. "'Bargains' . . . no, 'Deals . . . make it . . . safer . . . for . . . all . . . fools . . . to read lips. Three . . . twenty-seven . . . ninety-nine.'"

She lifted her head and frowned at her brother. "It's a bunch of nonsense, Josh," she stated flatly.

"I know," he mumbled, shaking his head. "I know. That's what I don't get."

She cocked her eyebrow. "I don't think there's anything *to* get."

"But the rest of the scroll isn't like that," he countered. "It makes sense, and it's really organized. It's divided into twelve parts—and each part is a prophecy about what happens in each lunar cycle of the year. Like for the first lunar cycle, it says, 'The sun will reach out and touch the earth,' just like Elijah told us on the bus. It says that the Chosen One will be separated from her brother. It talks about how this Demon will—"

"I *know*," Sarah grumbled, cutting him off.

She'd heard all of this already. She wasn't in the mood to hear it again.

"Just *listen!*" His voice rose. "Jesus, Sarah. Let me finish my sentence for once. See, every fourth block of words there's another little block of nonsense that has nothing to do with anything else in the scroll." He started carefully rolling up the exposed parchment. "*That's* what I'm curious about. And those numbers, too."

Sarah sighed. "Fine. So what do you think it all means?"

"I don't know." He shook his head. "Maybe it has something to do with the code Elijah was talking about. He said it was hidden in the scroll. . . ." He stared into space, as if he'd suddenly remembered something.

"Yeah?" Sarah prodded impatiently. "I'm listening."

He chewed his lip. "I don't know . . . Remember the time Elijah told us about the Bible Code?"

Sarah moaned. "Yes, Josh," she replied in a monotone. "He said that everything that has ever happened to anybody at any time is hidden in the Torah. I thought it was baloney then, and I think it's baloney now. So what's your point?"

He glared at her. "Why are you being such an ass? Don't you realize how *important* this is? Don't you get it yet?"

"Yeah, I *do* get it!" Sarah yelled. "I get that I have no idea what's going on. Do you really think we're gonna figure this out?" She threw her hands in the air, waving the knife over her head. "I don't even know what we're *trying* to figure out!" Impulsively she tossed the knife on the floor and snatched the scroll out of Josh's hands. "Here, let me see that thing—"

"Jesus, careful!" Josh whispered angrily.

"I *am* being careful," Sarah muttered. The scroll was pretty heavy, actually—heavier than she would have thought. She twisted the pegs, revealing another sea of black letters. How were they supposed to find a code in *that?* She shook her head, scanning the page. Almost every other word was *hashayd:* the Hebrew word for "the demon." The text was really pretty sick, now that she looked at it.

The demon betrays the false prophet. . . . The demon drinks blood and eats flesh. . . . The demon requires a burnt offering. . . .

She hesitated. *Offering.* Hadn't she heard that word somewhere recently? Yes—at Elijah's house. That eerie British accent came floating back to her: *"It will provide a fitting burnt offering for Lilith."*

"Who's Lilith anyway?" she found herself asking.

Josh shrugged. "I don't know," he answered distractedly. "There's no mention of a Lilith in what I've read so far."

She glanced up at him. "Do you think Lilith could be the Demon?"

Josh stared at her. "I don't—"

A deafening crash of glass erupted beside them.

On instinct Sarah ducked. Something sliced her hand. It took a moment of frozen terror for her to realize that the window had been smashed. Voices and footsteps suddenly filled the hall. A dark, crazed-looking boy in green fatigues was climbing through the shattered window frame.

Without thinking, Sarah bent for the knife on the floor—and found a pistol in her face.

"Stand up!" a voice commanded in Hebrew.

Sarah slowly straightened, still clutching the scroll. Her body was trembling uncontrollably. She glanced over her shoulder—and saw that Josh had a gun to his head as well. A fat boy in an identical green uniform was escorting him down the hall toward the opposite end of the building.

"Josh!" she called.

The crazed-looking boy shoved the muzzle of the gun against her temple and cocked the handle. "Silence!" he barked.

She held her breath. Josh vanished around the corner.

Oh, God—please don't let him get hurt. . . .

Three gunshots ripped through the air. Sarah plainly heard them whizzing past her head.

But much to her shocked surprise, the crazed-looking boy keeled over facedown on the floor beside her. A reddish black puddle oozed out from under his body.

What was happening? Why were they shooting each other?

Move! she commanded herself.

She ducked down under the window. "Josh?" she cried again. She snatched the gun off the floor, hugging the scroll next to her chest with her left hand. "Josh?"

He didn't answer.

There were several more gunshots, then silence. The footsteps and shouts faded. The attackers were outside now. She heard the roar of a truck's engine on the road in front of the barracks.

Summoning all her courage, she lifted her head just enough to peer out the window.

There!

A few uniformed kids were lifting her little brother into the green canvas opening in the back of a military truck. His body was limp, immobile. The kids hopped in after him. As soon as they were all inside, the truck sped down the road, disappearing in a cloud of dust.

"Josh!" she screamed. "Josh!"

But she knew her cries were in vain.

Her little brother was gone.

Official Rules
COUNTDOWN
Consumer Sweepstakes

1. No purchase necessary. Enter by mailing the completed Official Entry Form or print out the official entry form from www.SimonSays.com/countdown or write your name, telephone number, address, and the name of the sweepstakes on a 3" x 5" card and mail it to: Simon & Schuster Children's Publishing Division, Marketing Department, Countdown Sweepstakes, 1230 Avenue of the Americas, New York, New York 10020. One entry per person. Sweepstakes begins November 9, 1998. Entries must be received by December 31, 1999. Not responsible for postage due, late, lost, stolen, damaged, incomplete, not delivered, mutilated, illegible, or misdirected entries, or for typographical errors in the entry form or rules. Entries are void if they are in whole or in part illegible, incomplete, or damaged. Enter as often as you wish, but each entry must be mailed separately.

2. All entries become the property of Simon & Schuster and will not be returned.

3. Winners will be selected at random from all eligible entries received in a drawing to be held on or about January 15, 2000. Winner will be notified by mail. Odds of winning depend on the number of eligible entries received.

4. One Grand Prize: $2,000 U.S. Two Second Prizes: $500 U.S. Three Third Prizes: balloons, noise makers, and other party items (approximate retail value $50 U.S.).

5. Sweepstakes is open to legal residents of U.S. and Canada (excluding Quebec). Winner must be 20 years old or younger as of December 31, 1999. Employees and immediate family

members of employees of Simon & Schuster, its parent, sub-sidiaries, divisions, and related companies and their respective agencies and agents are ineligible. Prizes will be awarded to the winner's parent or legal guardian if under 18.

6. One prize per person or household. Prizes are not transfer-able and may not be substituted except by sponsors, in event of prize unavailability, in which case a prize of equal or greater value will be awarded. All prizes will be awarded.

7. All expenses on receipt and use of prize, including federal, state, and local taxes, are the sole responsibility of the win-ners. Winners may be required to execute and return an Affidavit of Eligibility and Release and all other legal docu-ments that the sweepstakes sponsor may require within 15 days of attempted notification or an alternate winner will be selected.

8. By accepting a prize, a winner grants to Simon & Schuster the right to use his/her name and likeness for any advertising, promotional, trade, or any other purpose without further com-pensation or permission, except where prohibited by law.

9. If the winner is a Canadian resident, then he/she will be required to answer a time-limited arithmetical skill-testing question administered by mail.

10. Simon & Schuster shall have no liability for any injury, loss, or damage of any kind, arising out of participation in this sweepstakes or the acceptance or use of a prize.

11. The winner's first name and home state or province will be posted on www.SimonSays.com/countdown/ or the names of the winners may be obtained by sending a separate, stamped, self-addressed envelope to: Winner's List "Countdown Sweepstakes", Simon & Schuster Children's Marketing Department, 1230 Avenue of the Americas, New York, NY 10020.